"You're here to h...

"Of course. I am Madiso...
River Bank hired me to h... ...bbing
their gold shipments."

Jericho stared at her.

"I believe you were expecting me?"

He snapped his jaw shut. The last thing he'd
expected was this frilly-looking female with her
ridiculous hat. In her green-striped dress and
twirling her parasol like that she made him think of
a dish of cool mint ice cream.

"Whatever is the matter, Sheriff? You have gone
quite pale. Are you ill?"

He jerked at the question. Not ill, just gut-shot. "Uh,
yeah. I mean, no, I'm not ill. Just...surprised."

She lowered her voice. "Most clients are surprised
when they meet me. It will pass."

Hell no, it won't.

* * *

The Lone Sheriff
Harlequin® Historical #1199—September 2014

Author Note

During my research for this book I was pleased to discover there were a number of women Pinkerton agents; in fact, Allan Pinkerton stated that some of his most valuable operatives, particularly during the Civil War, were women. So I thought a female agent in the Old West deserved her own story.

LYNNA BANNING

—

THE LONE SHERIFF

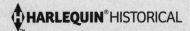

H HARLEQUIN®HISTORICAL

Recycling programs
for this product may
not exist in your area.

ISBN-13: 978-0-373-29799-3

THE LONE SHERIFF

Copyright © 2014 by The Woolston Family Trust

Printed in U.S.A.

For Joe Walsh, with love

With grateful thanks to:

Suzanne Barrett
Carolyn Comings
Kathleen Dougherty
Tricia Adams
Brenda Preston
Susan Renison
Ann Shankland
Austin Sugai
David Woolston

LYNNA BANNING

has combined a lifelong love of history and literature into a satisfying career as a writer. Born in Oregon, she has lived in Northern California most of her life. After graduating from Scripps College she embarked on a career as an editor and technical writer, and later as a high school English teacher.

An amateur pianist and harpsichordist, Lynna performs on psaltery and harp in a medieval music ensemble and coaches in her spare time. She enjoys hearing from her readers. You may write to her directly at P.O. Box 324, Felton, CA 95018, U.S.A., or at carowoolston@att.net. Visit Lynna's website at www.lynnabanning.com.

Prologue

TO: SHERIFF JERICHO SILVER, LAKE COUNTY, OREGON

SENDING TOP AGENT MADISON O'DONNELL TO ASSIST CAPTURE OF ARMED GANG STEALING WELLS FARGO GOLD SHIPMENTS

ALLAN PINKERTON
PINKERTON DETECTIVE AGENCY, CHICAGO, ILLINOIS

Chapter One

Smoke River, Oregon, 1873

"Sonofa—" Jericho shoved his shot glass of Red Eye around and around in a widening circle. That's all he needed, some citified armchair detective telling him how to do his job.

The bartender swept out a meaty hand and rescued the glass. "Got a problem, Johnny?"

"Nope. Gonna get rid of it soon as it turns up."

Jericho tossed off the whiskey and slapped the glass onto the polished wood counter. "No fancy-ass Pinkerton man from the city is gonna sit on his duff at the jailhouse giving me advice while staying out of the line of fire."

"Oh, yeah?"

"Yeah. Fill it up, Jase. Jawing with some city slicker from Chicago's gonna be easier with this inside me."

The bar man looked him over. "Ya keep this up, you're gonna be pie-eyed. That's your fourth shot."

Jericho grunted an obscenity. Pie-eyed was okay with him. Three weeks of chasing the Tucker gang, and now his arm was in a sling. His gun arm. He swore again and downed his shot.

The windowless saloon was smoky and dim, but it was over a hundred degrees outside and the Golden Partridge was the coolest place in town. He grinned at the paunchy man on the other side of the counter and slowly pivoted to study the room behind him. A puff of hot air through the swinging double door told him he was no longer alone.

Hooking his boot heel over the bar rail, he shoved both elbows onto the bar top and watched his still-wet-behind-the-ears deputy sidle up beside him.

"You gonna meet the train, Sheriff?"

Jericho nodded. The kid was young. Red-haired and shiny-faced, sharp as a whip and foolishly brave. Sandy had been with him two years, now. Jericho relied on him. Trusted him.

But Lake County had never faced anything like this before.

"Whatcha gonna do, Sheriff?"

Jericho shrugged. He had a plan, all right. At four o'clock this afternoon the big black steam engine would roll into the station and Madison O'Whatsisname would get off. At four-oh-five, Jericho would strong-arm him right back onto the train.

It'd be easy.

At precisely four o'clock, the Oregon Central chuffed into the station. Jericho adjusted his sling so the sheriff's badge showed, jammed his left thumb in his belt and waited.

The first person off the train was Darla Weatherby with her bossy mother-in-law right behind her. Another trip to the St. Louis opera house, he guessed; both women fancied themselves singers. Jericho had heard them once at a church social, warbling a duet in Italian. Lessons in St. Louis weren't gonna help.

After them came rancher Thad MacAllister, followed by old Mrs. Hinksley and her sister, Iris Du-Pont, both dressed in pink-checked gingham with parasols to match. Then came more passengers he didn't recognize, but none of them looked remotely like a Pinkerton man. A Pinkerton agent would no doubt be wearing a proper suit. But the only male who looked the least bit citified was Ike Bruhn, home from his honeymoon with his new bride.

Sandy jiggled at his side. "Ya see 'im?"

"Nope," Jericho grunted.

"Maybe he missed the train," his deputy suggested.

"Naw, must be here somewhere. Look for a gent in a gray suit." Pinkerton men always wore gray to blend in with crowds. He scanned the thronged station platform again.

"Check inside, Sandy. Maybe he slipped past me."

His deputy jogged off and Jericho perused the crowd a third time. Nothing. Maybe Mr. Detective had chickened out at the prospect of fingering an elusive outlaw gang that was robbing trains. He narrowed his eyes and was turning to check the station once more when someone stumbled smack into him.

"Oh, I am terribly sorry." An extremely pretty young woman carrying a green-striped parasol gazed up at him. Her voice sounded like rich whiskey sliding over smooth river stones, and for a moment Jericho forgot what he was there for. She only came up to his shoulder, and on her dark, piled-up hair sat the most ridiculous concoction of feathers and stuffed birds he'd ever laid eyes on.

He sucked in a breath to apologize, then wished he hadn't. Damn, she smelled good. Soap and something flowery.

Made his head swim.

He stepped back. "'Scuse me, ma'am."

She waved a gloved hand and peered at his chest. "Oh, you are the sheriff."

"Yeah, I am."

She smiled and his mouth went dry. "You are just the man I want to see."

Jericho swallowed. "You have a problem?"

"Oh, no." She twirled her parasol. "*You* have the problem. I have come to help." She waited, an expectant look on her face.

"Help?" Jericho echoed.

"Of course." The whiskey in her voice was now sliding over some pointy rocks. "I am Madison O'Donnell. The Smoke River Bank hired me to help catch the gang robbing their gold shipments."

Jericho stared at her.

"I believe you were expecting me?"

He snapped his jaw shut. He sure as hell wasn't expecting *her.* The last thing he'd expected was this frilly-looking female with her ridiculous hat. In her green-striped dress and twirling her parasol like that she made him think of a dish of cool mint ice cream.

"Whatever is the matter, Sheriff? You have gone quite pale. Are you ill?"

He jerked at the question. Not ill, just gut-shot. "Uh, yeah. I mean no, I'm not ill. Just…surprised."

She lowered her voice. "Most Pinkerton clients are surprised when they meet me. It will pass."

Hell, no, it won't.

Madison O'Donnell picked up her travel bag. "Shall we go?"

Not on your life. "Uh, my deputy's inside the station house. 'Scuse me, ma'am." He strode past her without looking back. Inside, he found Sandy talking to the ticket seller.

"Charlie says he hasn't seen anyone who looks like a—"

"No need. I've found him. Her," he corrected himself.

Sandy's rust-colored eyebrows went up. "Huh?"

"Madison O'Donnell. She's a 'she.'"

The deputy's face lit up. "Oh, yeah? A female? What kinda female?"

"A female kind of female," Jericho snapped. He headed for the doorway. "And don't spread it around about her being a Pinkerton agent."

"Gosh-a-mighty, Sheriff, what're you gonna do with a lady Pinkerton detective?"

"I'll think of something." He slammed through the entrance, Sandy in his wake, just in time to see the train rattle on down the track.

"Where is she, Sher—" His deputy's eyes widened. "Oh, criminy, she's mighty good-looking for a…" Sandy's voice trailed off. Jericho guessed young Sandy hadn't seen a woman like her before. A back-east woman with birds on her head.

He swallowed a chuckle, then turned it into a cough. Hell, he'd never seen a woman like her before, either.

"What're you gonna do with her, Sheriff?" Sandy said again.

"As little as possible. Close your mouth, Sandy."

Without another word, his deputy stepped forward and snagged the woman's travel bag. "Allow me, ma'am."

"Why, aren't you sweet! At least some of you men out here in the West have nice manners."

Sandy blushed crimson and spoke to Jericho under his breath. "I moved the extra cot into the jail like you said, Sheriff, but maybe… I mean, where's *she* gonna sleep?"

"I expect you have a hotel of some sort in this town, do you not? I will be staying there."

Jericho pointed down the main street to the white-painted Smoke River Hotel. Sandy took off at a jog, the travel bag bumping against his shin every other step.

"And, Sheriff Silver, I hope there is a dining room nearby? I ate a ham sandwich back in Nebraska and a day later I had an apple in Pocatello. Believe me, I am quite famished."

Famished, huh? She looked plenty well fed to him. Not for the first time, Jericho noted the swell of her breasts and the plain-as-day curve of her hips. Even without the bustle ladies wore these days, her backside was nicely rounded.

He stepped off the station platform and tipped his head after his deputy. "That way. Restaurant's near to the hotel." He gestured for her to precede him and they started single file down the main street.

Following her was pure misery. Her behind twitched enticingly and every male within fifty feet stopped dead and stared as she passed. Every last one of them pinned him with a you-lucky-son-of-a-gun look.

He caught up with her on the boardwalk and they walked in silence for exactly four steps. He noticed that her gaze kept moving from side to side, taking in everything, the dusty main street, the barbershop, the mercantile, even the honeysuckle along the fences. Her sharp eyes missed nothing.

"I am simply starving," she stated.

"You said that already. Dinner's up ahead." He pointed to the restaurant close to the hotel.

"First I shall register and check for any messages."

"Messages!" Jericho snorted. "Nobody's supposed to know you're here in Smoke River."

"Mr. Pinkerton knows. He will want a report every twenty-four hours."

Jericho snapped his jaw shut. Jupiter, he had a damn amateur on his hands. "A telegram can be intercepted—you ever think of that?"

"Why, of course. That is why I always send messages in code."

He clamped his teeth together and rolled his eyes. Code. That was a fancy back-east way of doing things. Out here in the West, you just plain *said* things.

Sandy waited at the hotel entrance, a dazed look in his eyes. Jericho gestured him inside. "She's gonna register. Tend to her bag, Sandy. I'll wait in the dining room."

"Gosh, thanks, Sheriff."

Detective O'Donnell breezed past them both, through the hotel entrance and up to the reception desk. Sandy glued his eyes to the lady detective's hip-swaying steps and Jericho swore under his breath. Clearly his deputy was already smitten. Young men were damn foolish.

He turned away, strode out onto the boardwalk and into the restaurant. "Bring me a cup of coffee, Rita. And add a shot of brandy to it."

The plump waitress eyed him. "Something wrong, Johnny?"

Without answering, Jericho headed for his favorite table by the window. "Make it a lot of brandy," he called over his shoulder. He had a bad feeling about this; the train back to Chicago didn't leave until noon the following day.

* * *

The dining room was crowded. Ranch owners and their wives, townspeople with their kids in tow—the room buzzed like a hive of bees. He settled in the corner facing the entrance and waited.

Rita brought his spiked-up coffee, and he waited some more. What took a woman so long to unpack a little bitty travel case? Or maybe she was upstairs decoding her messages. He swallowed a gulp of the black brew in his cup.

Sandy crossed the room, grinning like a Halloween pumpkin, and took the chair opposite him. "Got her all squared away, Sheriff." He tried to curb his smile. "She sure is somethin', isn't she?"

She was something, all right. She could be a lot of things, but one thing she was not was a Pinkerton detective. He could hardly wait to muscle her back onto the train.

Sandy stood up abruptly. "Here she comes."

"Right. Sandy, go on back to the jail."

Her entrance into the dining room caused a flurry of activity. When Detective O'Donnell glided into the room, every single male in the establishment rose to his feet, just like their mommas had taught them.

Jericho's momma hadn't taught him a damn thing. Jericho's momma had dumped him at the Sisters of Hope orphanage in Portland and forgot he even existed. He never knew whether she was white, Indian, or Mexican, though his bronzy skin suggested one of his parents was something other than white.

Miss O'Donnell darted over to him. He rose automatically because that's what the nuns had taught him. She grabbed his hand and yanked hard.

"What the—"

"Never, *never* sit by a window, Sheriff. Surely you know that?"

"Well, sure I know that, but I'm not exactly on duty."

He lifted his trussed-up right arm. "Got shot up."

"Of course you are on duty. A good sheriff is always on duty." She tugged him to an empty table in the far corner of the room. "Sit with your back to the wall," she whispered. "Always."

"Oh, for crying out— Look, Miss O'Donnell, you fight your war your way and I'll fight mine like I've always done." He dropped into the closest chair.

"It's *Mrs.* O'Donnell," she shot back, sinking into the opposite chair. Her eyes snapped. For the first time he noticed the color, a green so clear and luminous it looked like two big emeralds floating under a cold, clear stream.

"Sorry. Didn't know you were married." Somehow that had never occurred to him.

"I am not married, Mr. Silver. I am a widow."

He blinked. "Sorry," he said again.

"Do not be sorry," she sighed. "I was never so bored in all my life as when I was married."

Bored? She was bored doing what all women dreamed about from the time they were in pigtails? Before he could pursue the subject, Rita appeared and quietly slipped Jericho's forgotten cup of coffee onto the table near his left elbow. Detective O'Donnell peered at it with an avid look.

"Please, would you bring me what he's having?"

Rita frowned, then caught Jericho's eye. "You don't mean exactly like his, do you, Miss?"

"Of course I do."

"Just make it plain coffee, Rita," he directed.

Mrs. O'Donnell's green, green eyes flicked to his cup and then up to meet his. "Make it *exactly* like his, please."

Rita raised her graying eyebrows and darted another glance at Jericho. "*Exactly* like yours, Johnny?" she murmured.

Jericho tried not to smile. "Yeah, exactly." He'd teach Miss—Mrs.—City-bred Detective not to make assumptions about things in the West.

Mrs. O'Donnell's coffee came almost immediately. Rita hovered near the table, and Jericho knew why. The detective's coffee had to be at least half brandy, and Rita wanted to watch the lady swallow a mouthful.

So did Jericho. He followed the lady detective's every move as she picked up the cup with a small white hand and blew across the top. Then she downed a hefty swallow.

He waited.

Nothing. No choking. No coughing. No watery eyes. Instead, she dabbed at her lips with a dainty pink handkerchief and took another mouthful.

Still nothing. He couldn't stand it any longer. "Taste okay?"

"Certainly. That is surprisingly good brandy. Made from cherries, is it not?"

Chapter Two

Rita rolled her eyes, slipped away and returned with dinner menus. Before she could get her notepad out of her apron pocket, Mrs. Detective started talking. "I'd like a big, juicy steak, rare, and lots and lots of fried potatoes. Extra crisp."

Maddie watched the sheriff seated across from her. His frown brought his dark eyebrows close to touching across the bridge of his nose.

"Same for me, Rita." He folded both menus with his left hand and handed them back.

Maddie studied his hand—long, tanned, capable-looking fingers and a muscular wrist. An odd little twang of something jumped in her chest. She always made it a point to notice hands; this man's said a great deal about him. For one thing, he used them a lot outdoors. And for another, he didn't fidget like so many men did in her company.

When their steaks came, Sheriff Silver took one look at her heaping plate and his eyebrows went up. "You eat like this all the time?"

"Oh, no. But I do love steak. My mother's French cook served nothing but chicken breasts drowning in fancy sauces. Now I eat steak every chance I get, pan fried, broiled, even baked. I never grow tired of the taste."

The sheriff said nothing, but she noticed he managed a surreptitious glance at her waistline. He did not believe her. Probably he did not believe she was a Pinkerton agent, either. She calmly cut into her steak and forked a bite past her lips.

She chewed and swallowed while he stared at her. "Are you not hungry, Sheriff Silver?"

He looked down at his untouched plate. "Guess not. Guess I'm feeling a bit off with you here."

"But you knew I was coming." Maddie's arrival on an assignment for Mr. Pinkerton often elicited such a response. She had learned to disregard it and get on with the job she was hired to do.

"There's 'knowing' and 'knowing,' Mrs. O'Donnell. I sure as h—sure as hens lay eggs wasn't expecting anything like you."

"Mr. Pinkerton selected me especially for this assignment. It will be easier to disguise my purpose in Smoke River. Being a woman, I mean."

He fanned his gaze over her body again. "There's not a way in hell to disguise that fact, Mrs. O'Donnell. Seems Pinkerton didn't think this all the way through."

She watched him study her face. *Oh, my.* The sheriff's eyes were such a dark blue they looked almost black. And tired. And mysterious in a way that made her knife hand tremble.

She laid her shaking hand in her lap. "Mr. Pinkerton always thinks things through. A woman can be in plain sight and still be in disguise. No one will question a female being in your company."

"Yes, they will," he said. "I'm pretty much known as a loner around these parts. A woman in my company, especially one like you, will have tongues wagging all the way to Gillette Springs."

"Not if I am your sister, on a visit." She picked up her knife.

"Not possible."

"Oh? Why not?"

"I was raised in an orphanage. I've no idea who my parents were, save that they were in a hurry to get rid of me. So I don't have any sister, and the whole town knows it."

Maddie thought for a long moment. "Your cousin, then. We will tell people I am your cousin."

"My cousin!" His left hand jerked and his fork skittered off the table.

"Once removed," she purred.

Rita appeared, rescued the sheriff's fork and supplied another. "Want me to cut up your steak for you, Johnny?"

He grunted. The waitress made quick work of the sheriff's meat and retreated to the kitchen. He speared a bite left-handed, then swigged down a gulp of coffee.

Again she noticed something unusual about him—the way he handled his coffee cup. He turned the handle away from him and picked it up by covering the top with his fingers and lifting up by the rim. He slurped in the liquid between his thumb and forefinger. But he never took his eyes off her face.

"If you are my cousin," she admonished, "you should stop looking at me like that."

He clanked the cup onto its saucer. "Like what?"

"Like you have never laid eyes on me before."

He stared at her. "Shoot, lady, I *haven't* laid eyes on you before."

Maddie swallowed. She had never encountered anyone like this man. He was tall and he moved quietly, like a big cat she'd seen in the zoo once. He was short-spoken to the point of rudeness. He was amusing in a backhanded sort of way. He was…fascinating.

"Well, Cousin…Jericho, should we not get acquainted?"

"Acquainted?" He frowned.

"Of course. To start with, my given name is Madison. Maddie for short."

"Maddie."

She watched his mouth when he said her name. She liked it best when his lips opened for the "mah" and she glimpsed straight teeth so white they looked like fine fired china from England.

"Cousin or not, Mrs. O'Donnell, I don't need you."

"Oh, but you do. I have observed that you have been wounded and cannot use your right hand. I am here not only to cover your back but to serve as your gun hand."

"No, you're not," he grumbled. "Tomorrow you're getting on the train back to Chicago."

"But you cannot—"

"Try me."

His lips were not as attractive pressed in the thin straight line they were in now.

Rita popped up to take their plates. "Like some dessert tonight? Got some fresh rhubarb pie, Johnny."

"No, thanks."

"Rhubarb!" Maddie's mouth watered. "My mother's cook made rhubarb pies every summer. I would simply love a piece of pie. A big one."

The sheriff's eyebrows did their little dance again.

"And a scoop of ice cream on top, please."

The sheriff looked at her as if she had cotton bolls growing out her ears. "You don't like rhubarb?" she asked.

"Love rhubarb. Just lost interest in the idea right now. We were talking about the train to Chicago."

"*You* were talking. I was not."

"Look, Mrs.—Cousin Madison—"

"Maddie," she reminded.

"The Tucker gang's not just dangerous, they're mean. All five of them are escaped convicts, and they're desperate."

Her coffee cup paused midway to her mouth. "Do you know their identities?"

"Only one of them. Tucker. I saw the whole gang once, after they pistol-whipped a train engineer so bad he couldn't see for a month. Saw their dust when they rode off, and counted five horses."

"Did you recognize any of the horses?"

"Yep. All stolen from the Bevins ranch up north. Didn't see the gang again until the next gold shipment was stolen."

"Is that when your arm was injured?"

"Yeah. I was on the train, but just as I got to the mail car, one of them fired on me. Bullet caught my wrist."

She fished her notepad and pencil out of her reticule. "And how long ago was that?"

"Eight days. Why all the questions if you're leaving in the morning?"

"Sheriff Silver...Jericho." She smashed her spoon into the scoop of vanilla ice cream on top of her piecrust. "The Smoke River bank manager hired me for a reason, Sheriff. I have a job to do and I intend to do it. The last thing—the very last thing—I am going to do tomorrow is leave."

A forkful of rhubarb-stained ice cream disappeared past her lips.

Jericho sat back in his chair and stared at the woman across from him. What she was doing to her ice cream was exactly what he felt like doing as well, only not with a slab of pie.

"I don't need you, Mrs. O'Donnell."

"I am not leaving tomorrow," she replied calmly. Her lips, he noticed, were colored rhubarb pink.

"Yeah, you are."

"No," she said calmly, "I am not. For one thing, with your arm in a sling you are not strong enough to force me onto the train. And for another, you do need me. I am a crack shot."

She couldn't be. She was full of baloney and a liar to boot. He had to get rid of her before she got all tangled up in something she didn't know squat about and got herself hurt.

The thought sent a knife into his gut, a knife he'd thought long since forgotten.

"You realize I could have my deputy arrest you."

She just grinned at him. "Your deputy is already swoony over me. He would never arrest me."

Well, damn. He couldn't let her stay. She could be dangerous to have around. He couldn't shoot straight enough left-handed to protect himself, let alone protect her, too.

Somehow he had to scare her off.

"Listen, lady, I don't know any way but blunt, so here it is. It's no dice. You'll get us both killed."

"I would not. I would be an asset."

"Don't kid yourself. I'd spend more time looking after you than catching up with Tucker. I can't risk it."

Her eyes flared into green fire. "You mean you *won't* risk it. All outlaw chasing is risky and every Pinkerton agent accepts that. I did not take you for a coward, Sheriff."

Jericho stared at her. She could sure talk a blue streak. Pretty convincing, too, with her chin jutted out like that and those ivy-colored eyes boring into him.

He massaged his chin. "You wouldn't be a help, lady. You'd be a damn nuisance."

She stabbed her fork into the center of her ice-cream-soaked pie. "Would you care to bet, Mr. High and Mighty? Within the next fifteen minutes, I will prove my worth to you. And when I do," she added in a voice that could cut glass, "you can buy my breakfast tomorrow morning. Is it a deal?"

Hell's bells, she made him so mad he couldn't think straight. "If you're finished mauling that pie, I'll escort you to your hotel room."

She laid her fork down with deliberate care. "I said, is it a deal?"

"Deal," he bit out.

She scooped up the last mouthful of rhubarb-flavored ice cream and folded her napkin beside the plate. "Seeing me to the hotel won't be necessary, Sheriff."

"Don't argue," Jericho shot back. "We're not in Chicago, ma'am. In this town at night it's necessary."

Once outside the dining room, she marched along beside him, talking a mile a minute while Jericho clenched his teeth.

"What a pretty little town this is." She gestured across the street. "Just look at all those lovely green trees."

He grunted. She might talk a lot, but again he noted her gaze was always moving, taking in everything from the street to the boardwalk to the storefronts.

Jericho only half listened to her chatter. "...in

Philadelphia, where I was raised…and then Papa… I guess you could say that I ended up in a fancy cage with a rich, very dull banker. Just when I couldn't stand it one more minute, he caught pneumonia on a sleigh ride and made me a widow."

She paused for breath. "My goodness, what smells so sweet?"

"Honeysuckle. Along the boardinghouse fence." He gestured with his sling arm, then winced.

"Do you think the owner would mind if I picked some for my room? What heaven, to smell that delicious fragrance all night long."

"The owner is Mrs. Sarah Rose. Lost her husband at Antietam. She won't mind, she picks it herself when somebody's ailing or havin' a baby."

She stepped off the boardwalk and darted across the street to the white picket fence. From somewhere she pulled out a tiny pair of scissors. After a few delicate snips, she returned to his side clutching a straggly bouquet in her gloved hand.

"Oh, look, there's the mercantile. I must visit the mercantile, and I must find a dressmaker, as well."

Jericho groaned. A woman could spend hours in the mercantile choosing flower seeds or fabric or… whatever women bought. He followed the lady detective inside, where the proprietor, Carl Ness, slouched behind the counter reading a newspaper. At the sight of Maddie, he straightened up, ramrod stiff.

Jericho didn't like the way Carl was staring at her, but Maddie seemed unperturbed. Her gaze scanned each shelf.

"Have you any scented bath soap?"

Carl sent Jericho a puzzled look. "What kinda scent?"

"This is Mrs. O'Donnell, Carl. She's my…"

Maddie turned her attention to the proprietor. "Gardenia is my favorite. Have you any gardenia-scented soap?"

"Nope."

"What about carnation?"

"Nope."

She bit her lip. "Heliotrope? Rose?"

"All I got is lavender, ma'am. Take it or leave it."

"I will take half a dozen cakes. Large ones."

Jericho bit back a laugh. Half a dozen! She'd be the cleanest person in Smoke River.

Carl wrapped up her purchase in brown paper and tied it with string. "Anything else?"

The answer was immediate, and for a moment Jericho thought he hadn't heard right.

"Yes. Three boxes of thirty-two-caliber cartridges."

Carl stared at her, then turned his widened eyes on Jericho. "That all right with you, Sheriff?"

Hell, no, it wasn't all right. Damned fool woman, what did she think she'd do with bullets, hold up the hold-up gang?

Maddie didn't wait for his answer. "Double-wrap them, please. So they won't get wet."

"Wet?" Jericho exploded. "You gonna go swimming on your way back to Chicago, *cousin?*"

"Of course not. But it might rain while I—"

"Hold it!" Jericho had had enough for one night. "We're goin' back to the hotel. Now."

"But what about the dressmaker?"

"What about her? Name's Verena Forester and she opens up at eight o'clock every morning. Your train back to Chicago leaves at noon."

Jericho smiled. Maddie practically spit sparks when she was mad. Before he knew it, she'd latched on to his good arm and drawn him off to one side.

"I absolutely must see the dressmaker," she whispered. "Tonight, if possible. I am, well…out of… some things."

"Huh?"

She rolled her eyes. "I…um, I have no extrasmall clothes," she intoned. She waited a beat. "You know, camisoles and bloomers and…things."

He stonewalled.

"Lingerie," she muttered.

He enjoyed baiting her. He also enjoyed imagining what her lingerie looked like. Silky, with lace? "How come you've got no underthings?" he asked blandly.

"My valise was lost when I changed trains in St. Louis. All I have with me is a very small travel case, and it carries only the minimum garments. So you see—"

"Tough."

"Really, Sher—Cousin Jericho," she murmured. "What would Aunt Bessie say about that?"

"Bad luck, I guess. Who's Aunt Bessie?"

"My mother."

Jericho almost laughed out loud. "*Aunt Bessie*

would probably say 'plan ahead.'" He looked up at the ceiling and noted the avid interest of the mercantile owner.

"Come on, let's vamoose." He pulled her toward the door.

"Hey," Carl yelled. "What about my money?"

"Put it on my tab, Carl. Cousin Maddie always pays me back."

Outside the heat had diminished, though the night air was still warm and soft. Jericho drew in a deep breath and blew it out slowly, looking up at the stars. Hell, he'd like a drink. Talking Mrs. O'Donnell out of something was like pushing a pig into a pillowcase. She was nosy and outspoken and attention-getting, and he'd be glad when she was gone.

In silence they started back to the hotel. Up ahead, Jericho spotted Lefty Dorran in the alley between the mercantile and the barber shop. Lefty was a big overgrown almost-man, and Jericho had arrested him twice this summer for assault. He caught the glint of metal and instinctively put Maddie on the other side of him.

Too late. Lefty had a sharp eye for a pretty woman, and even the fact that she was walking with the sheriff didn't deter him. The kid burst out of the alley onto the sidewalk and sidled up to her.

Jericho tried to block him with his left shoulder, but Maddie stepped to one side and then faced the towering hulk with a perfectly serene expression on her face.

Lefty kept coming. Maddie neatly stepped into

his path, pivoted on one foot and swept her other leg around behind him. Then she hooked the toe of her shoe around the back of his knees. The next thing Jericho saw was Lefty's hulking body sprawled face-down in the street.

Maddie dusted off her white gloves and smiled up at him. "I told you I would prove you needed me. You owe me one breakfast. Eight o'clock sharp."

All the way back to the hotel and up the stairs to Room 14, Jericho thought over what she had just done. Didn't seem possible that a slim woman like Maddie had laid that big galoot out flat. Some kind of Oriental trick, maybe. Lord, the woman was down-right dangerous.

At her hotel room door she slipped the key into the lock and turned to face him, her soft-looking mouth quirked up in a smile.

"It has been a most interesting evening, Sheriff. I would not have missed it for anything."

"Sure wish I could say the same, ma'am."

"Good night, Cousin Jericho. Do get some rest. You are looking quite peaked."

Chapter Three

"Sheriff? Sheriff, wake up!"

Something joggled Jericho's shoulder. "Go 'way," he mumbled.

"Can't, Sheriff. You gotta wake up."

Jericho cracked open one eyelid to see his deputy standing over him. The kid better have a good reason for breaking into a damn good dream.

"Why do I?"

"Sorry, Sheriff. Maybe you forgot you're s'posed to meet that detective lady for breakfast?"

Jericho shot upright and instantly regretted it. His temples pounded and he snapped his lids closed against the bright light. "You sure?"

"Eight o'clock, Sheriff. Least that's what you said last night. But that was before—"

"Yeah? Before what?" The kid's face seemed kinda out of focus.

Sandy studied his boots. "Uh, before you polished off that bottle of whiskey."

Jupiter, now he remembered. Sort of. His head throbbed and his mouth felt as dry as an empty well. And his stomach—

He'd think about his stomach later. He dragged himself off the cot and pulled on jeans and a clean shirt. He'd skip shaving; he couldn't really focus on anything, much less see his face in the mirror. Besides, it was hell to shave left-handed.

"She sure is pretty."

"Who?"

"Miss O'Donnell. Sheriff, didn't cha even notice?"

"Don't get your hopes up, son. It's *Mrs.* O'Donnell. And she's leaving on the noon train."

Sunshine poured through the front windows of the restaurant like the eye-stabbing beam of a lighthouse. God help him, he could barely see through his slitted lids.

He spotted Mrs. Detective perched primly at the corner table, spooning sugar into her coffee.

"Good morning, Sheriff."

He winced. Did she have to sound so cheerful?

"Mmm-hmm," he grumbled. He took the chair across from her, facing away from the glare. Rita appeared at his elbow.

"Coffee," he managed.

Maddie looked up. "I will have three eggs over easy, bacon cooked very crisp, fried potatoes and some ketchup, please."

Jericho's stomach heaved at the description. "Just coffee, Rita," he repeated. "And could you please bring it in the next sixty seconds?"

The plump waitress must have sensed his desperation because an entire pot immediately appeared before him, along with an oversize mug.

Jericho eyed Mrs. Detective through the steam rising from his cup. There was something annoying about a woman who looked this trim and tidy at breakfast. And this pretty. She sent him a wide smile and, without thinking, he nodded.

Big mistake. Any motion made his vision blurry and his head… He groaned. His head felt like a railroad crew was laying track between his temples.

She pulled out her notepad and pencil and plopped them onto the tablecloth beside her. "Well, Sheriff, would you care to hear my observations thus far?"

Jericho blinked. "Observations? You mean what you've learned so far about the Tucker gang?"

"Oh, no. I mean in general. It's always wise to gather background information, don't you agree?"

He gulped down another mouthful of the scalding coffee. "Okay, let's hear it."

She flipped open the small leather-covered book. "First, your deputy—Sandy, is it?—is too sensitive to be much help on this mission."

Too sensitive? Exactly what did that mean? Did she think he was going to feel sorry for the outlaws? He gripped the coffee pot handle in a stranglehold and refilled his mug.

"Second, Mr. Ness, at the mercantile, does not like you."

"Doesn't take a genius to figure that out. Carl doesn't like anybody much. Even his wife."

"Has there been trouble in the past between you and Mr. Ness?"

"Yeah. Small stuff, mostly. He sold me a sack of moldy potatoes once, and I confiscated a shipment of some Chinese herb he ordered because it was half opium."

Mrs. Detective nodded and went on. "Third, the hotel manager is cheating the Mexican couple who brought up my morning bath. Fourth—" She broke off and looked him over so thoroughly he wondered if his hair had gone curly overnight.

"You look awful, Sheriff."

"Didn't sleep much." And he'd drunk more last night than he had in a dozen years.

"It appears to me you are not yet awake."

Jericho snorted. He was awake enough to notice she smelled good, like lavender. "Is that your fifth observation?"

"My fourth, actually. My fifth observation is that there won't be another Wells Fargo gold shipment until Tuesday."

"Tuesday," he repeated. He already knew that, but he was impressed that she'd talked to the bank manager already this morning. He wondered if she'd also visited the dressmaker.

That thought led to a consideration of her underclothes. Were they brand spanking new? Or maybe she wasn't wearing any? *Don't go there, you damn fool.*

"Yes, Tuesday," she said. "That is tomorrow."

Thank goodness, the coffee was kicking in. "I

wouldn't worry about it, Mrs. O'Donnell. You'll be on the train going the other direction. Back to Chicago."

And then he could get back to the plan he'd already laid out.

"I most certainly will not be." She twiddled her fork until Rita laid a plate heaped with food in front of her. The smell of cooked bacon replaced the lavender fragrance and Jericho began to feel nauseated. He poured another mug full of coffee.

"I've got good reasons for sending you back, Mrs. O'Donnell. Care to hear 'em?"

"Certainly," she retorted. She grasped a thick slice of bacon between a delicate thumb and forefinger and crunched it up in two mouthfuls.

Jericho tried not to watch. "First, you're a woman. And being female and pretty fine-looking, that means you're gonna draw attention wherever you go."

"Pish-posh." She stabbed her fork into the yolk of one fried egg. "I know how to disguise myself."

Jericho had to look away from her plate. He'd sure like to see a disguise that would cover those curves. Even wearing a feed sack, she'd still look awful damned attractive.

"Second, you're a woman. That means you're not as strong as either me or my deputy, no matter what kind of fancy Chinese wrestling you can do."

"Japanese. Judo is a Japanese art." She stuffed a forkful of fried potatoes into her mouth.

"Third…" Jericho held up three fingers on his left hand—at least he hoped it was three. "You're a woman, like I said, and that means you don't think logically. Also you jump to conclusions."

Her fork clanked onto her plate. "You are either misinformed about the capabilities of the female members of the species or you are just plain prejudiced."

"I'm prejudiced," he growled. "Fourth, I'm the sheriff here, not you. And on top of everything else, you don't take orders well."

An odd expression flared in her green eyes and Jericho unconsciously held his breath. After a tense silence, she folded her hands in her lap and her lips opened. "I have been told that over and over since I was three years old, and it is true. I do not take orders well. But I *do* take orders, provided they make sense and are halfway reasonable. However, I warn you those are big ifs."

Jericho pressed on. "Fifth, you talk too damn much."

She looked up from her breakfast, her eyes wide. "What?"

"I don't talk much," he offered. "I've got to ride the train to Portland to intercept the gang, and that train takes six hours. I don't guess I could stand more'n about an hour of your note-taking and observations and jabber."

Her face turned crimson. "Jabber! Why you arrogant, pigheaded, incapacitated, sorry excuse for a lawman. What makes you think I could stand an hour of your moody, bad-tempered silence?"

He delivered his final shot slowly, making every

syllable count. "Let's face it, Mrs. O'Donnell, we're mismatched. The bottom line is we're not about to partner up, and I'll make it plain why not." He made his voice as growly as possible. "You're too much trouble."

He could scarcely believe what he saw next. Huge, glittery tears rose in her eyes and hung trembling on her lower lashes.

"I do not care one whit if we are mismatched," she said in a carefully controlled voice. "I am a professional detective. I have accepted an assignment. And I will follow through on it or I will die trying."

Calmly she forked a bite of fried potato into her mouth.

Jericho seethed inside while she chewed and swallowed, her eyes still shiny with moisture. Good God, he could take a woman's sobbing, even screaming, but tears that didn't go anywhere, that just sat there like diamonds on her dark lashes, tore him up inside.

"Okay. Okay, Mrs. O'Donnell. You win."

Her head snapped up and she glared at him.

"Madison," she amended. "My given name is Madison but I prefer Maddie."

More glaring. Hell's half acre, now her eyes looked like chips of green ice.

"Okay, okay." He wrapped her nickname around his tongue. "Maddie."

She looked into his face for a long moment, and when she opened her mouth to let words fall out, her voice was so quiet it was like snow drifting onto a meadow.

"Damn right," she said.

Jericho clenched his jaw. She had guts, he'd say that for her. She had other things, too, but he was trying like the devil not to notice.

He dragged his attention away from her soft-looking mouth. "Tomorrow's train to Portland, with the gold shipment aboard, leaves at eight o'clock sharp. In the morning," he said with emphasis.

"Thank you, Jericho." She tried a thin smile, but it wavered out of her control. "I will be aboard."

Chapter Four

At ten o'clock that night, Jericho crawled into his bed cold sober. He'd be up and bushy-tailed at dawn, and by seven o'clock he'd be on the train to Portland with forty thousand dollars in gold from Wells Fargo stashed in the mail car. Miners from all over Oregon and even Idaho brought their diggings to the Smoke River Bank, trusting they would safely ship it to the vault in Portland. And Jericho would be on board that train to make sure their diggings stayed safe.

Alone.

He hated to lie. It was one of the things he'd sworn he'd never do. Lying made him less of the man he'd wanted to be ever since he was twelve years old and on the run from the Sisters of Hope. Back then, he'd resolved he would always face up to the truth.

He lay on his narrow cot behind the sheriff's office and tried not to flinch at the deception he'd laid for Mrs. Detective, telling her the train departed at eight o'clock when it actually departed at seven. First, he'd stopped in at the hotel and found that Mrs. O'Donnell had left a wake-up reminder at the desk. He'd suspected as much; she was the type who planned all her moves ahead. In exchange for agreeing not to arrest the hotel manager's seventeen-year-old son for peeking in sixteen-year-old Lavonne Cargill's bedroom window, the manager obligingly tore up Mrs. O'Donnell's wake-up reminder note.

Next. He'd visited the mercantile for some pain-killer. A skinny kid he'd never seen before lounged against the cash register, studying Jericho's sling. "For yer arm, huh?"

"Yeah. Not too much laudanum—makes me drowsy. Where's Mr. Ness?"

"Home, I guess. I'm his cousin from Idaho. Name's Orion."

Jericho nodded. He didn't look much like Carl. "Been here long?"

"'Bout two weeks. Stopped here on my way to strike it rich."

"Gold mining?"

"Nah. Selling Red Eye to the miners up in Idaho." He scrabbled on the shelf behind the counter and produced a small bottle of dark liquid. "This stuff is mostly alcohol. How much of it do you want?"

"All of it." He needed to start exercising his stiff wrist and limbering up his gun hand, and he knew it would hurt some.

The kid wrapped up the bottle and Jericho stuffed it into the inside pocket of his deerskin vest. Funny the way Orion handled the bottle—with his pinkie in the air like a lady lifting a teacup.

The last thing Jericho did before crawling onto his cot that night was slip off his sling and stretch his arm out straight. Made his wrist hurt like hell, but he managed eight stretches in a row.

Before first light, he rolled off the cot, downed a cup of Sandy's gritty, cold coffee, and grabbed his gun belt. His deputy slept in the concrete-block jail in whatever cell was vacant. Jericho felt fine leaving the kid in charge; the jail was empty.

On his way to the train station he studied the second-floor windows of the hotel; dark as the inside of a barrel. He felt a stab of guilt, but he squashed it down and smiled instead. Mrs. Detective would sleep right on past train time. Kinda mean to trick her, but he knew he couldn't tolerate sitting next to her for six hours.

And, he admitted, there was more to it than that. He couldn't stand to see a woman get hurt, especially not one he felt responsible for. The Tucker gang could be vicious.

The train was already puffing smoke out the stack as he swung himself aboard and entered the passenger car.

What the—

Maddie O'Donnell sat in the first seat, smiling at him like a self-satisfied fox with a chicken in its belly.

"What the hell are you doing here?"

She patted the faded red velvet cushion next to her with a gloved hand. "We settled all that yesterday, Sheriff. There is no need to go through it again."

He couldn't help staring at her. She wore a different hat, yellow ribbons with flowers and a veil rucked up on top. A crisp yellow ruffled skirt boiled around her ankles and a lacy yellow shirtwaist was tucked into as trim a waist as he'd ever seen. She looked like one of those daffodils that poked up each spring in the orphanage garden.

Her outfit looked brand-new. He wondered if her underclothes were new as well. He forced his gaze away.

The train lurched forward and Jericho grabbed onto the upholstered seat back. Maddie swept her skirt aside to make room for the sheriff beside her. He did not sit down for the longest time, just stood swaying in the aisle, staring at her. What on earth was he looking at? Oh, of course—her new hat. True, it was too gaudy, but it added to her disguise. Besides, once Mrs. Forester, the dressmaker, had warmed to the idea of the flowers, it was hard to stop her. The woman had grumbled at being roused at such an early hour, but Maddie had purchased enough clothing to make it well worth her while.

Carefully, she unpinned the creation, ripped off all but three daisies, and resettled it atop her pinned-up hair. She secured it with her longest hatpin; it was also the sharpest of her collection. In a pinch, it made an effective weapon.

"Why do you not sit down, Sheriff? I promise not to talk."

He frowned down at her. "Don't want to muss up your skirt, Mrs. O'Donnell."

"You won't. It's made of seersucker. Wonderful fabric for traveling on an assignment—it never wrinkles, no matter what I do."

The train picked up speed and swung around a sharp curve, and the sheriff edged onto the seat as far away from her as he could get.

Maddie huffed out a breath. "You do not like me much, do you?"

His eyes—a dark, inky blue—flicked to hers for an instant, then dropped to the boots he'd stretched out and crossed in front of him. "Not much, no."

She pursed her lips. "Tell me something, Sheriff."

He did not answer.

"Why are you so unfriendly?"

The sheriff gave an almost imperceptible jerk, and then he turned those eyes on her. Now they looked angry. Almost feral.

After a long silence he started talking, his voice so low she could hardly hear him. "Don't really like most people."

"But whyever not? What has happened to make you so…well, surly?"

"I watched a friend die in my place," he gritted. "After that, I didn't like being close to anyone."

Maddie blinked. "Who was he?"

He looked past her, out the train window, and she watched his gaze grow unfocused.

"She."

"She? Your…?" Maddie hesitated. He was so

rough around the edges she doubted he'd ever been married. A lover, perhaps? She was keen to know, but it would be highly improper to ask. She said nothing, just noted the tightness around his mouth.

"She, uh, died for something I did."

"Why, that is perfectly awful! How old were you then?"

He shrugged. "'Bout ten, I guess. I never knew for sure what my age was."

Maddie's throat felt so raw she could scarcely speak. She closed her eyes. How he must have hated himself. She would not be surprised if he still did. She shut her mouth tight. What could she say to ease a scar like that? Nothing.

He recrossed his legs. "Heard enough?"

"More than enough," she breathed. It explained everything, his brusque manner, his hard exterior, the unreachable part of himself he kept shuttered.

He slipped the sling off his arm, flexed his wrist, and waggled each of his fingers individually. Some of them, she noticed, seemed reluctant to move.

"Does that hurt?"

"Hell, yes, it hurts."

"Then why—"

"Because I'm gonna need a steady gun hand and a trigger finger that works, that's why."

Go ahead, she thought. *Grumble and roar all you want.* She was not going to let herself be intimidated by him.

He said nothing for the next hour, just worked his wrist and his fingers back and forth, his lips thinned over his teeth. Perspiration stood out on the part of his forehead she could see; his black hair straggled over the rest.

The uniformed conductor stuck his head into the car. "Next stop Riverton," he yelled.

Two passengers boarded, an old man, bent nearly double and a young woman, probably his daughter, who held on to one of his scrawny arms. She settled him four seats behind.

The sheriff gave them a quick once-over, then reattached his sling and pulled a small bottle from inside his vest.

"Pain medicine," he said to no one in particular.

"What you drink is your business, Sheriff."

He gave her a long, unblinking look. "Damn right."

Maddie laughed out loud, then clapped her hand over her mouth. Jericho swigged a mouthful from the bottle, corked it and stowed it in his vest pocket.

"Now, Mrs. O'Donnell, What about you?"

"Me! What *about* me?"

The ghost of a smile touched his mouth. "What happened to you that makes you so sure of yourself and so stubborn?"

"N-nothing. It just comes naturally. My upbringing, I suppose."

"Ladyfied and spoiled, I'd guess."

Maddie bit her lip. "Well, let's just say rich and protected. Actually, overprotected. My mother was English, very high society. My father was Irish and very well-off. A banker."

"Figures," Jericho muttered.

"I married young to get away from them, really. He was also a banker. After a while—a very short while—I realized my husband was only interested in my money and he only wanted a wife for a show-piece. So I became just that—a china doll with pretty dresses. It didn't take long before I wanted a real life."

He snorted. "What the hell is a 'real life'?"

She thought for a long minute. "I am not sure exactly. Someone who loves me for myself. Real friends, not society matrons. At least I know what it is not—finishing schools and servants and a closet full of expensive clothes."

He took care not to look at her, staring again out the window at the passing wheat fields. "Seems to me, Mrs. O'Donnell, that you're gonna feel kinda lost out here in the West. Ought to be back in the big city, where you belong."

She turned toward him. "I suppose I do feel lost, in a way. The West is so…well, big. Things— towns—are so far apart."

"Yeah, that spooks a lot of Easterners."

"But I do not feel lost when I am on an assign-ment for Mr. Pinkerton. Then I know exactly who I am. It makes me feel…worthwhile."

She pulled a ball of pink cotton thread from her travel bag and began to crochet. Her fingers shook the tiniest bit.

Jericho leaned back and closed his eyes. Noth-ing more worth saying, or asking, he figured. He must have dozed for hours and suddenly the train screeched to a stop. A glance through the window told him they were not in a train station; they were out in the middle of nowhere.

Hell's bells, here it came.

Left-handed, Jericho dragged his Colt out of the holster, thumbed back the hammer and started for the mail car. A swish of petticoats at his heels told him Maddie was right behind him.

"Stay here," he yelled over his shoulder.

"Try and make me!"

Damn fool woman. She'd get herself killed and he'd kick himself to hell and back. He wished he'd never laid eyes on her.

In the mail car, the white-faced clerk stood frozen, hands in the air, while a man with a bandanna covering the lower half of his face held a revolver on him with one hand and, with the other, hurled a canvas Wells Fargo bag through the open side door.

Maddie darted off to Jericho's right, clutching a revolver.

"Get down!" he shouted. The young mail clerk dropped to the floor but Maddie went into a crouch and leveled her weapon at the robber.

"Hands up!" Her ordinarily genteel voice cut like cold steel.

The man straightened in surprise, then turned his gun toward the voice. Jericho sent a bullet zinging off the silver handle and the gun skidded across the floor in front of Maddie. She stopped it with her small black shoe and kicked it into a corner.

Three men on horseback waited outside the car. Maddie swung her pistol toward the opening and fired, winging one man. Another outlaw pointed his weapon at her but Jericho's shot spun it out of his hand.

The mounted robbers began peppering the wall behind them with gunfire while the man inside ducked and began shoving more canvas bags out onto the ground.

A tall rider with a paunch walked his horse up to the car and took careful aim at Jericho, but before he could squeeze the trigger Maddie fired a shot that neatly spun his weapon out of his hand. Where had she learned to shoot like that?

Fat Man reined away. Maddie sent another bullet through his flapping black coattail.

The man inside skedaddled after the canvas bags, shoved one more off the car and then tumbled out onto the ground after it. He dove under his waiting horse. Jericho itched to shoot him, but with his left-handed aim off, he figured he'd kill the horse before he nailed the outlaw.

The three others hefted the canvas sacks behind their saddles, mounted and thundered off in a cloud of gray dust. The last man scrambled onto his horse and pounded after them.

Jericho raised his revolver to pick him off, but he was out of range.

Maddie put a shot through his hat, but he twisted in the saddle and fired back at her. She yelped.

The bullet tore through the sleeve of her shirtwaist, burning a path above her elbow. It felt like something scraping her skin with a white-hot knife.

Then there was nothing but dust, the audible prayers of the crouching mail clerk, the chuff of the train engine, and Jericho yelling at her.

"Dammit, Maddie, you'd think you'd be smart enough to stay out of the line of fire!" He leaped over the clerk and grabbed her arm. Right where it hurt.

She gritted her teeth. "If you do not let me go, Sheriff, I am going to shoot you, too!"

He snatched his hand away and stepped back, eyes narrowed. "Are you hurt?"

She lifted her arm and pointed to the black-rimmed hole in the sleeve. "Bullet burn."

He opened his mouth again. She was sure he was going to yell at her some more, but she interrupted. "Sheriff," she enunciated quietly.

"What?"

"Shut up."

He looked dumbfounded. "What?"

"Be quiet. I am not seriously injured and I see that you are unharmed, as well." She began to gather up the disordered mail bags.

"Hell," Jericho muttered. "You're not even shook up."

She pocketed her pistol. "Stop complaining and help me."

He looked at her as if he'd never seen her before. "How come you're not shakin' or cryin' or something?"

Maddie straightened, gripping one corner of a heavy canvas bag. "Why should I be?"

Jericho shook his head. "How much do you figure they got away with?"

Maddie cocked her head. "How much?" She found she liked teasing him. It made his eyes even darker blue, and the way he was staring at her now caused a little flip-flop inside her chest.

"How much?" she repeated. "Well, to the best of my calculation—did I tell you I was a whiz at mathematics at school? Let's see now…"

He planted himself within spitting distance and propped his good hand on his hip. "I'm waiting, dammit."

"The amount of money—" she smiled into his glowering face "—is exactly zero."

"Huh?"

"You heard me, zero. Nothing. *Nada. Rien.* Those Wells Fargo bags are decoys. The bank manager and I decided they would be filled with rocks, not gold."

His eyes went even darker. "You mean this whole exercise was just a farce?"

Maddie straightened her skirt. "You could call it that, I suppose."

"Then what the hell did we risk our lives for?"

"For observation." She dropped the canvas bag in her hand, which landed with a clunk, and fished her notebook out of her pocket. Not her Pistol Pocket, he noted, but the Observation Notebook Pocket.

Jericho waited while she circled the pencil around like a branding iron. Part of him wanted to laugh.

Another part of him wanted to wring her neck. He'd be damned if he'd risk getting shot for some damn decoys!

"Well," she began, a note of relish in her voice. "We got a good look at the robbers, didn't we? There are five of them."

"We already knew that."

"One of them," she continued, "is lame. His leg is stiff."

"And?"

"And one of them wore a bandanna from Carl Ness's mercantile. I recognized the pattern and the color, a sort of pinky-red. Did you notice?"

Jericho said nothing. He had to admit she had sharp eyes and a keen mind. Her "observations" were valuable.

Dammit, anyway.

The trembling mail clerk slid the railcar door shut. The train tooted once and jerked forward. Maddie stumbled and bumped his injured wrist. He sucked in a breath. Hurt like blazes.

With his good hand he holstered his Colt and turned back to the passenger car. "Better let me take a look at your bullet burn," he said as they made their way down the aisle.

She plopped down into her seat, pressing her lips together. "No, thank you. The bullet just skimmed my arm. I'm sure the skin is not broken."

He settled beside her with an exasperated sigh. "Yeah? Show me."

"No."

He reached for her wrist. Before she could stop him he'd unbuttoned her sleeve and pushed it up above her elbow.

"Hurt?"

"Yes," she said tightly.

He ran his gaze over her slim upper arm, noting the angry red crease above her elbow. From his inside vest pocket he grabbed the bottle of painkiller.

"What is that?" she said.

"Painkiller. Alcohol, mostly."

She rolled her eyes. He uncorked the bottle with his teeth, lifted her elbow away from her body and dribbled the dark liquid over the abrasion. Her breath hissed in and she moaned softly.

Jericho closed his eyes for an instant. He hated hearing a female in pain. "Sorry."

"It is quite all right," she said, rolling her sleeve down. She poked her forefinger through the bullet hole and sighed. "Another visit to the dressmaker, I suppose."

"Maddie, maybe you ought to see a doctor when we get to Portland."

She shook her head. "What is that you poured over it?"

He recorked the bottle. "I told you, painkiller. For my wrist."

She gave him a lopsided smile that made his insides weak. "We are a pair, are we not?" she said, her voice just a tad shaky. "A one-armed sheriff and a Pinkerton detective with a bullet burn."

"Yeah," he said drily. "We're a team, all right. Listen, Maddie, tomorrow I think you should go back to Chicago."

"No, you don't, Jericho. Whether you admit it or not, you need me. This is my job—apprehending lawbreakers. I'm your right arm, so to speak, so you're stuck with me."

He felt more than "stuck" with her. He felt bowled over. Something told him his lady detective wasn't going to back down and go home to Chicago anytime soon. Torn between worry over her safety and his need to see this job through, his insides were in an uproar.

With a sidelong glance at her, he settled back to think about how he could keep her alive while he did what he had to do, apprehend the Tucker gang. The townspeople always wanted him to get up a posse, but Jericho preferred working alone. Always had and always would. He did what any sheriff worth his salt had to do, and he'd never wanted to get anyone else involved.

And he sure as hell didn't want to get a lady detective mixed up in a manhunt, even if she could shoot straight. She had to go back to Chicago.

She picked up her crocheting again and worked a row of stitches before she said anything more. "Do you suppose there might be an opera or a play of some kind in Portland?"

"Might be. You miss the city, huh?"

"Yes," she said. "To be honest, I enjoy cultural things."

"Bet you feel like a fish out of water on this assignment."

"Oh, no. I am not that easily discouraged. This fish likes doing something worthwhile, Sheriff. Catching train robbers is worthwhile."

Jericho nodded. He felt the same way, when he thought about it. He had a job to do. But he'd been on his own since he was a kid, and that's how he liked it. Wasn't responsible for anybody's skin but his own. Every time Sandy begged to come along on a manhunt, Jericho neatly evaded the issue.

He liked Sandy. Maybe that was the problem. He was beginning to like Maddie, too, and that was an even bigger problem.

Chapter Five

To calm her nerves Maddie paced up and down the passenger car aisle until Jericho glared at her. She would never admit to the sheriff how shaken she felt after her encounter with the train robbers, but there it was. She'd come close to being killed for the first time in her career as a Pinkerton agent. Mr. Pinkerton had trained her in the use of firearms, but he'd used her to carry messages and smuggle maps, nothing so violent as being caught in the middle of a gun battle.

After four round trips from the back of the car to the front, she sank onto her seat. Still jittery, she hunted up the wooden crochet hook and resumed work on her edging. Jericho sat next to her, exercising the fingers of his right hand.

Was his heart pounding as hard as hers was? She shot a look at his impassive expression and almost laughed. If it was, he hid it better than she did.

The train jerked, and her ball of crochet thread rolled down the aisle, leaving a trail of pink string.

She huffed a sigh and began to rewind it, but the ball settled into a crack in the floor.

The sheriff stopped flexing his injured wrist, got to his feet and chased the ball of thread into a corner. He snatched it up, stomped back and dumped it into her lap. Then he plopped back down in his seat without saying a word.

Well! He had no right to be angry with her. She had probably saved his life; he might at least say thank-you.

The train rolled smoothly forward through wheat fields and cattle ranches. The peaceful scenery soothed her to the point where she could review the events that had occurred in the mail car. One thing she couldn't forget was the look on the sheriff's face when she'd first drawn her pistol, part shock, and part fear. She could understand his surprise, but fear? She would bet a barrel of fancy hats this man didn't fear outlaws or anything else.

And then suddenly she understood. He feared for *her*.

Maddie laid her hands in her lap. "I had no idea you could shoot left-handed. Why did you not tell me?"

"You never asked. You just jumped to a conclusion. That's another reason why you should skedaddle back to Chicago, you jump to conclusions."

"Oh, no, it isn't. That is not why you don't want me along. Is it?" She pinned him with eyes as hard as green stones. *"Is it?"*

He waited a long time before answering. "Nope."

"Then would you tell me what the real reason is?"

"Nope."

She waited. The train picked up speed and the car began to sway. "Sheriff, I deserve to know. I am waiting."

"Okay," he growled. "Here it is in plain English. *You* are the reason I don't want you along."

"Oh, for mercy's sake! Sheriff Silver, you are irritating enough to drive a person crazy."

He gave her a tight smile. "But not irritating enough to drive you away."

She blanched. "Well, of course not. It would take more than a stubborn, bad-tempered, set-in-his-ways man to make me give up on an assignment."

"Damn," Jericho muttered. What *would* it take, he wondered. He couldn't forget the picture she'd made in that yellow dress, firing her shiny pistol at armed outlaws. He knew she'd been covering his back, and he should be grateful. A wrong-handed sheriff was no match for outlaws with revolvers.

But deep inside, where he never allowed himself to venture, something began to tighten. God, he hated that. Made him sweat. He couldn't let her continue with this Pinkerton business. If she didn't get him killed, she'd get herself killed, and that would be even worse.

Two hours passed in uneasy silence. Maddie crocheted carefully on what looked like a lace edging; Jericho tried not to watch her slim fingers.

"Last stop, Portland," the conductor boomed. "Ten minutes."

Maddie smoothed out her skirt, shook her petticoat ruffles into place, and stowed her crochet work
in her oversize reticule. "What do we do until the
train leaves for Smoke River?"

"Find a hotel."

"A hotel!" Her eyes went wider and even more
green. "What do we want a hotel for?"

"Don't know about you, but I'm grabbing an early
dinner and getting some sleep."

She eyed him with a look that could fry eggs.
"You mean we are stuck here in Portland? *All
night?*"

"Yep. Train east doesn't pull out until tomorrow
morning. Thought you would have researched that,
Mrs. Detective. Distances out here in the West are…
long."

Maddie set her jaw. She was hungry, she admitted. And bone tired. But the worst part was that she
was surprised at this turn of events. She hated being
surprised. Back in Chicago, trains ran both east and
west every hour. Somehow she thought trains out
here would run every hour, as they did in Chicago.
It never occurred to her the distance between Smoke
River and Portland would mean an overnight stay.
Why, she hadn't even brought a night robe.

The streets of Portland were jammed with people—
merchants, travelers, ranchers with wagons full of
children, some fancy men who looked like gamblers,
ladies driving trim black buggies, townspeople,
schoolboys, even a few dusty-looking Indians. After

battling the crowds, Jericho stepped into the foyer of the Kenton Hotel with Maddie at his elbow.

The desk clerk looked up and thumbed through his registry. "'Fraid I got no rooms left, mister. Big carnival from San Francisco in town and we got lotsa visitors. You could try the Portland Manor, just across the street."

The Portland Manor had only one vacancy. "Two beds, take it or leave it. Town's full up."

Jericho turned to her. "That okay?"

Maddie stared at him. "You don't mean one room for the two of us?" she whispered. "Together? Why, that is scandalous!"

"Huh! That's real funny coming from a lady who said she was bored to death with her marriage."

"But—"

"Look, Mrs. O'Donnell, my arm is hurting like a sonofa—billion beeves. I'm worn out and hungry enough to eat just about anything. We're here, and we're staying. Like the man says, take it or leave it."

"But—"

"And," he added with a lopsided smile, "you can relax. I'm too flat-out tired to threaten your virtue."

Her cheeks went pink. "This is highly unusual. Mr. Pinkerton will certainly hear about it."

"No, he won't. You let one word slip about our arrangement and I'll tell Pinkerton it was all your idea."

Maddie turned crimson, then white, then crimson again. "You would not dare!"

"Try me."

Stunned into silence, Maddie watched him sign *Mr. and Mrs. J. Silver* on the register. She wanted to protest, but everything was all so mixed up and tense between the two of them that…well, she would just have to act as if things like this happened every day to a Pinkerton detective and make the best of it. For her next assignment she would research geographical distances more thoroughly.

The hotel room was small but clean, with a single chest of drawers, washstand, armoire and two narrow beds jammed in an arm's length apart. Jericho surveyed it and smiled inside. Wasn't every day he got to sleep next to a pretty woman, even if it was in a separate bed.

"It'll do," he said as nonchalantly as he could manage. "It's been a long day. Come on, let's go have some supper."

He downed two more slugs of pain remedy before entering the hotel dining room and, as he ate, his steak seemed to taste more and more delicious and the stale coffee less bitter. How much laudanum was in this pain stuff, anyway? Even Maddie's stiff silence was less annoying.

Fact was, even bone tired with an arm that throbbed, he was beginning to feel pretty good. Who cared if she wanted to keep quiet? It was a rare woman who could talk a blue streak most of the time but keep her mouth closed when it was necessary. He had to give her some credit.

The waiter removed their plates and brought more coffee and some tea for Maddie. "You folks going to the carnival? Got some real pretty gir—uh, horses, I hear."

"Horses?" Maddie's eyes took on a sparkle he hadn't seen before.

Jericho wasn't interested in the girls the waiter tried not to mention, but horses? That was another matter. No matter how weary he felt, he always liked looking at good horseflesh.

"Oh, could we?" Maddie begged. "Please?"

He stared at her. He'd never heard her use the word "please" before. So the city girl liked horses, did she? Well, why not have a look?

The Summer Carnival was a six-block section of the main street, blocked off at either end. Admission was a nickel, and Jericho gallantly dropped two nickels into the burly ticket taker's palm, one for him and one for Maddie.

She nodded her thanks. "Where are the horses?"

"Yonder." The man tipped his graying head over his shoulder. "Behind the gypsy fortune-teller."

Maddie wheeled in the direction indicated and started off down the walkway. She was in such a hurry, Jericho found he couldn't keep up with her. He trailed her past the green-painted ice-cream stand and a man poking flaming swords down his throat to a roped-off area where a half dozen horses waited patiently for riders.

"Oh," Maddie breathed. "How beautiful they are!"

He'd never heard such awe in her voice, but he had to agree. "Probably from a ranch nearby. They'd never look this good if they'd been herded up from Sacramento, or even shipped by rail."

Maddie caught his good arm and pointed. "Look at that one, with the cream-colored mane."

He'd been looking at that animal; she was a beauty, all right. A mare, maybe three or four years old, a golden-tan color with cream mane and tail. "You've got a good eye for horseflesh, Maddie."

"In addition to the bank, my father owned a fancy riding stable in Chicago. All the society ladies took equestrienne lessons."

Jericho moved in close to the palomino mare, let her smell his neck and chest.

"I do want to ride him."

"Her," he corrected. "Mares don't have—" He swallowed the rest. "Sure, if you want to."

She sidled up next to the horse and cautiously laid one finger on its nose. Then she looked up at Jericho with a yearning in her eyes that made his stomach flip.

"Could I really ride him? Her, I mean?"

The wrangler led the animal to the center of the roped-off corral. "She's real gentle, Miss. You ever ridden before?"

"N-no, not much. My father never allowed me to ride."

"Well, then, your man here can hold the rope so's the mare can step real slowlike in a circle around him."

Jericho walked her close to the animal and raised

one knee so she could mount. "Put your foot here, Maddie, and I'll boost you up."

"Boost me? Is that proper?"

He laughed. She was one citified lady, all right. "Probably not," he intoned for her ears only. "But seein' as how we're sleeping together…"

She sent him a dark look, then edged closer. Gripping his bad arm, she lifted her tiny little shoe onto his knee and he hoisted her up. He kinda regretted that she didn't need more of a boost to her posterior; he enjoyed laying his hand on that nicely rounded behind.

His elbow gave a sharp twinge, which he ignored. The wrangler tossed him the lead rope and Jericho led the mare in a circle around the ring. Maddie kept a death grip on the saddle horn, but she made quite a picture in her pouffy hat and yellow shirtwaist, even with a black-rimmed bullet hole in one sleeve.

She rode around him a dozen times. Every so often she freed one hand and leaned forward to tentatively pat the mare's neck.

"Good girl. Good horse. My, you are beautiful. You look like a big dish of coffee ice cream with caramel sauce."

Jericho laughed out loud. After her last circuit she drew back on the reins and the horse stopped. "How do I get down?"

He dropped the lead rope and strode toward her, intending to hold out his arms. Oh, damn, he remembered he didn't have two arms. Instead, he reached up and slid his good hand around her waist.

"Bring your other leg over the saddle and then jump down." He gave her a little tug.

She went pale, but she lifted her leg over the saddle. Her skirt kicked up, revealing a froth of petticoats, and when she slid off she stumbled hard against him. For just an instant he felt her soft breasts brush against his chest.

Lord in heaven.

"Oh, that was wonderful," she cried. *"Wonderful."*

Jericho groaned. He thought so, too, but it wasn't the horse he admired. It was her.

Maddie practically danced out of the corral. "Such a beautiful animal. You simply cannot imagine how happy riding her makes me!"

Jericho blinked. "You're that happy about a horse?"

"Oh, yes. I sense a kindred spirit in the animal."

"That never happened before?"

"No. Never. As I said, Papa never let me visit his fancy riding stable. I'm going to call her Sundae."

"Kinda odd to fall in love with a horse, Maddie." He meant it as a joke, but her face immediately looked grave.

"All my life I have felt different. Alone. Even when I was married." She gave a little half sob. "Then," she said in a voice so low he could scarcely hear her, "it was even worse."

Jericho nodded. He knew what she meant. In fact, he knew exactly what she meant, but he was sure surprised at her words. "Yeah, I can understand makin' friends with a horse. Glad you enjoyed it."

Well, yes and no, Jericho admitted. He found himself a mite irritated at her feelings for the animal. Almost as if he was…

Jealous? Of a horse? *Get a grip, mister. This woman is not yours.*

He'd never been a fool about a woman and he wasn't about to start now, especially with this one. Ever since he'd lost his friend Little Bear, he'd kept his heart protected inside a safe, sturdy iron cage.

Maddie drifted to the fortune-teller's tent, a red-and-gold India print with a hand-lettered sign pinned to one flap: Madame Sofia, Gypsy Fortune-Teller.

Maddie was already seated at the scarf-draped table across from the wrinkled old woman and was stretching out her palm.

He tried his darnedest not to listen, but one word sliced into his brain like a shard of glass. *Chicago.*

Maddie rose from the table, an odd look on her face. "Your turn, Jericho. Let Madame Sofia tell your fortune."

"What for? I can pretty much see my life from here on out." He'd be a good sheriff and he'd never get involved with a woman. At least, not until he was too old to care.

Maddie sped across the grass to his side. "I dare you."

She tugged on his good arm.

Damn, she was more persuasive than he'd bargained for. Finally, shamed into it, he seated himself before the gypsy woman, slid his right arm out of the sling, and opened his hand, palm up. The old woman bent over it, stroking the lines with her gnarled forefinger. After a moment she looked up into his face.

"You have known great sorrow," she said in her gravelly voice. Then she reached out and touched his face. "What comes will not be easy."

"What won't?" he said without thinking.

The gypsy smiled. "This." She cut her gaze to where Maddie waited.

His face set, Jericho paid the gypsy and propelled Maddie away from the tent. Twenty yards further, he stopped with a jerk and gazed upward.

"What the hell is that?" He squinted to read the signboard. "Turkish Up-and-Down Wheel."

Directly in back of the sign stood the strangest contraption he had ever seen, a grid of steel bars with a bucket-type seat at each end. A man in baggy pants and a pointed red hat cranked on a gearlike arrangement; as the bars turned, the seats rose up and then came slowly down.

"Oh, look! Could we...?"

"Could we what? Ride that thing? Probably break both our necks."

"Oh, please? Just this once?" She sent him a pleading look.

Damn, she was sure hard to refuse. Jericho shrugged and moved into the ticket line. A few minutes later they were side by side in the cushioned tublike seats, and the wheel began to rotate with squeaks and groans. Their seat swung high above the carnival grounds.

Maddie caught her breath. She could see for miles,

across the entire city with its street lamps, the tall, lighted buildings, the bridges arching over the smooth-flowing river spread out below her.

"Isn't that just beautiful," she sighed.

He laughed and she was amazed. She had never heard him laugh before.

"More beautiful than your horse, Sundae?"

"More beautiful than anything. It feels as if I can see the whole world and all the little lives down below. It makes me feel…hungry. And…" She hesitated. "Sad, in a way."

Jericho stared at her. It was getting harder and harder to see her as a Pinkerton agent from Chicago. Maddie O'Donnell was looking more and more like a young, pretty woman who was warm and alive and just plain human.

On the other hand, she knew some fancy Japanese judo moves and she could shoot a pistol accurately enough to flip a man's weapon out of his hand. She wasn't like any young, pretty woman he'd ever laid eyes on.

The chairs creaked and dipped and rose again. "You are a puzzle, Maddie."

She twisted her head toward him. "Really?"

"Yeah, really." He looked away, focusing on the tiny carnival lights far below.

"Am I not measuring up?"

Hell, she measured up, all right. Worse than that, he was beginning to like her. God, that was the last thing he wanted to do.

"It's not that," he said slowly. "You're plenty brave.

And you're damn smart. You could probably shoot the sulfur tip off a matchstick with that shiny pistol of yours, but…"

"But what? You must admit I *have* helped. Just a few hours ago I kept you from taking a bullet in your back.

"Okay, Mrs. Detective, it's like this. I don't want to be grateful to you. I don't want to be obligated to you for anything. I don't want to need you along with me and I sure don't want to enjoy your company."

Which he did, he admitted. More than he wanted to.

"Well, then, what *do* you want?"

Good question. "Damned if I know."

"What does that mean, exactly? Have you changed your mind about me? About having me along?"

"Hell, no."

"Well, what, then? I deserve an answer, Jericho. An honest one."

"Okay, here's an honest answer. I want to… I want to keep you safe. I don't want to feel responsible for you."

She turned away, her eyes shiny, and suddenly he regretted every word he'd said. Maybe he'd hurt her pride.

It shouldn't matter, he told himself.

But it did.

Chapter Six

The climb up the hotel stairs seemed interminable with Maddie swaying enticingly ahead of him. If he quickened his pace he could reach out his hand and—

"Will the horses still be there tomorrow morning?"

Jericho checked his step. "Dunno. You want another ride on Sundae?"

"Yes," she breathed. "I most certainly do. I was never allowed to ride astride in Chicago. My mother said it was unladylike." Her voice sounded so wistful he felt his heart pinch.

She reached the door to their hotel room and patiently stood aside while he turned the brass key in the lock. When the door opened, she pushed inside and waited while he lit the oil lamp on the bureau. Their shadows jumped on the wall.

In the soft light Maddie studied the two quilt-covered beds, then sat down on the one nearest the window. "I'll take this one."

"Good," he grunted. "I want the one closest to the door."

She lifted her head. "Why?"

He closed the door and clicked the bolt closed. "An old habit, I guess. From the orphanage."

"Oh? Tell me what happened at the orphanage."

Hell's bells, this woman was full of questions he didn't want to answer. "It has to do with my friend at the orphanage, the one I told you about."

"Yes? What about your friend?"

Jericho swallowed hard. "My friend slept next to the window. I always took the cot next to the door. To get to her they had to deal with me first."

"Why would anyone want…?" Her voice trailed off.

Jericho moved slowly through the room, bounced his good hand on the bed and plopped down. "Little Bear was always getting into trouble."

"Little Bear, that was your friend's name?"

"She was the only friend I had at that damn place, and I wanted to protect her."

"But you were only ten years old." A thoughtful look came over her face. "What happened to Little Bear?"

Jericho's jaw clenched. "I'd rather not talk about it."

"Tell me," she urged. "Tell me, please."

He opened his mouth twice and each time decided he couldn't do it. He'd never told a living soul about Little Bear; maybe it was time he did.

"Little Bear was an Indian kid. Shawnee. About

nine years old, I guess. Came to the orphanage about the same time I did, but the nuns didn't much like Indians. They didn't much like me, either, so Little Bear and I got to be friends. Good friends."

He stopped and shut his eyes.

"And?"

"One day I stole an apple pie from the kitchen, and we were eating it out behind the garden when they caught us. They blamed her because she was an Indian. Took her out in the yard and whipped her." He swallowed again. "She never made a sound."

Maddie's hand went to her throat. "My goodness," she breathed. "What happened then?"

Jericho took a double breath. "She died the next morning."

He turned away from the horrified look in her eyes and bent to shuck his boots. He had to do something, anything, to get that memory out of his mind.

"Oh, Jericho, that must have been awful."

"Yeah, well, I lived through it. She didn't. I've never been able to forget it."

Maddie closed her eyes. What could she say to ease a scar like that? *Nothing.*

He stood up. "Heard enough?"

She nodded once, lifted off her hat and began to pluck tortoiseshell hairpins from the bun at her neck. Her hair came down in a tumble of dark waves; it looked so shiny and silky-soft all at once he wanted to run his fingers through it.

He had to turn away. "I'll, uh, use the facilities

at the end of the hallway." He escaped out the door and into the passageway. He strode back and forth in front of the door to slow his pounding heartbeat and clear his head, then eventually stepped back inside the room.

Without asking, he walked to the nightstand and blew out the lamp. In the blackness, softened by the glow of light from the hotel across the street, he gulped the last of his pain medicine and tossed the empty bottle into the wastebasket. Then he started to unbuckle his gun belt, but his hand stilled. He hadn't thought about how to get his clothes off with her in the room. He'd bet she hadn't considered that, either.

Tough luck. She wanted to play at being his partner? Maybe this was a way he could scare her back to Chicago. He dropped the gun belt to the floor with a thud then unsnapped the metal buttons of his jeans. Damn hard with only one hand.

He heard her shoelaces sigh through the metal eyelets, then a thump—another thump—and the rustle of petticoats. "I cannot believe I am doing this," she said suddenly. "Undressing in a hotel room… with a man."

"Me, neither." Too late he wished he'd suggested they sleep in their clothes.

"Jericho, were you ever married?"

"Nope."

"Why not?"

"None of your business," he said drily.

He slipped off the sling and shrugged out of his

vest and shirt, but he left his drawers on. Didn't feel right getting completely naked with her in the room.

The room was airless and hot. "Maddie, open the window, will you?"

When he heard the sash slide up, he folded the quilt back all the way to the bottom of the bed and stretched out on the cool top sheet. She'd be about down to her pantalets and camisole now. He closed his eyes.

She made an odd sound and he realized she was struggling out of her corset. Laced up the back, didn't they? He hadn't spent much time with calico girls, but he thought he remembered, even though on those occasions he hadn't been exactly sober.

He stared up at the ceiling, trying not to listen.

At last the muffled sighs and swishes stopped and there was silence except for the sound of breathing— hers quick and light, his deeper and slower. Much slower. He couldn't help wondering what she looked like peeled down to her nothings.

It was going to be a long night.

"Jericho? Are you awake?"

His breath hitched in. "No."

"When did you leave the orphanage?"

"I lit out when I turned twelve."

"That must have been difficult."

Yeah, it sure as hell had been, but he didn't feel like elaborating. He had to change the subject. "What were *you* doin' when you were twelve?"

"Playing tea party with my dolls and learning French."

"Real tough childhood, huh?" He was sure glad she couldn't see his face in the dark. He had an idea what it looked like; when he scowled, kids gave him a wide berth.

"If women had the vote, young ladies could have more useful lives."

He thought that one over. "If women had the vote, maybe their *men* would lead more useful lives."

"That does not follow," she said. Jericho gritted his teeth. He couldn't think up good answers to her nosy questions this late at night.

"Maddie?"

"Yes?"

He rolled his tense body toward the door, putting his back to her. "Shut up and go to sleep."

She laughed softly. "The same to you, Sheriff."

At the first faint blush of pink light outside the window, Maddie popped her lids open. "I am going back to the corral at the carnival to say goodbye to Sundae," she announced.

Jericho opened one eye. "No, you're not. You'll miss the train back to Smoke River."

"I thought you didn't want me along?"

"I don't. But I don't want you stranded in Portland with no protection, either."

"I don't need your protection."

"Yes, you do, Mrs. O'Donnell."

"And," she said triumphantly, "with your injured arm, you need mine."

He groaned and closed his eyes. "Go back to sleep, Maddie."

An hour later, a shaft of sunlight fell across his face and he sat bolt upright. Must have drifted back to sleep after his before-dawn conversation with Maddie.

He glanced at the lump in the next bed and let out a sigh of relief. For once, she'd taken his advice.

"Time for breakfast," he announced.

No answer.

"Remember, the train leaves at eight."

No answer.

"Maddie, wake up!"

Silence.

Oh, damn. He shot over to her bed and flipped off the covers. Instead of Maddie he found a pillow patted into a sausage shape. Mrs. Detective was gone.

Hurriedly he splashed water over his face, ignored his two-day growth of beard and threw on his clothes. Never dressed so fast in his life.

She had to be downstairs in the dining room. Had to be.

But she wasn't. He had an uneasy feeling he knew where she was; he'd bet a month's wages she'd sneaked off to see that horse. Dammit, he'd warned her about catching the train!

He seethed inside, but he wasn't about to go after her. Damn headstrong, maddening, single-minded woman. She could starve for all he cared.

"Coffee," he barked at the waiter. "You see a young woman in a yellow dress earlier this morning?"

"'Fraid not, mister. You're our first customer today."

Jericho pulled out his pocket watch and glared at the numerals. Quarter to eight. Jumpin' jellybeans, the train.

"Skip the coffee. Let me have a dozen biscuits." Damn her hide. After a few minutes the flustered waiter handed him a brown paper parcel and Jericho headed for the train station.

The train sat on the eastbound track, engine puffing clouds of black smoke. He climbed onto the iron boarding step, hung on with his good arm and craned his neck, watching the platform for a ridiculous daisy-covered yellow hat.

Nothing. Passengers brushed past him, some carrying suitcases and picnic hampers, some with children trailing after them. Two undertakers in shiny black suits squeezed past him and one frail old woman with a limp approached. He stepped down and reached out his good hand to help her up onto the landing.

"Thanks, sonny," she rasped. She disappeared into the passenger car and Jericho again turned his gaze to the station platform.

Still nothing. Two minutes until eight. He narrowed his eyes against the morning sunshine and scanned the platform again. And again. By God, he'd strangle her.

All at once the train lurched hard and began to roll slowly forward. He hooked his good arm around the steel handhold and leaned his body out as far as he dared to give one last look.

There she was! Just stepping onto the platform. The engine gave a shrill toot and he caught a glimpse of her surprised face.

"Maddie," he yelled. "Hurry up!"

She caught up her skirt in one hand and with her oversize reticule clutched in the other she began to race alongside the moving railcar, her petticoat frothing around her ankles.

The engine started to speed up. Jericho slipped the sling off his right arm and stuffed it into his pants pocket. Anchoring his left elbow around the curved metal handhold, he leaned out and reached toward her with his right hand.

Damn, that hurt.

Her face white and frightened, she strained to catch up, stretching one arm toward him. Jericho leaned out another precarious inch and touched her fingertips.

One more inch…just one more inch. He lunged for her wrist and wrapped his fingers tight around it. With his right arm he pulled with all his strength and suddenly she tumbled against him. He grabbed her around the waist.

"Gotcha."

Her face was pressed into his neck and he felt her warm breath puff in irregular gusts against his neck. She tried to say something but she was so out of breath she could only pant.

He dragged her with him up one step and back onto the jolting platform between the railcars, yanked open the passenger-car door with his left hand, and shoved her inside.

His right wrist felt as if someone was chopping at it with an ax.

Maddie collapsed into the first empty seat and sat bent over her knees, gasping for breath. Jericho brushed the biscuit parcel to the floor and sat down hard beside her. She clung to her heavy reticule so hard her knuckles were white. He pried her fingers from the chain and lifted the bag out of her grasp.

Still unable to talk, she shook her head and grabbed it back.

The relentless pain in his right wrist and hand hammered at him. He scrabbled in his vest pocket for the painkiller, then remembered he'd finished it off last night. Still panting hard, Maddie snapped open her bag, drew out a greenish bottle of something, and thrust it at him.

"What's that?" Whiskey, he hoped.

She shook her head, still unable to get a word out, and pointed to his aching wrist.

"Painkiller?"

She nodded.

"You almost missed the train for this? Of all the dumb, irresponsible, feather-headed things to do—"

"Not…that," she gasped out. "Said…goodbye to… Sundae…first."

His first impulse was to laugh, but somehow

he couldn't. She'd risked missing the train back to Smoke River to bring him some more painkiller? Something inside his chest tightened into a knot.

"Damn woman," he muttered. "Almost had an apoplexy when you didn't show up."

She nodded again and held out the green bottle. He didn't feel up to arguing about it so he uncorked the stopper and took a long pull. It was mint flavored and felt real hot going down.

"Thanks, Maddie. I mean it. My wrist hurts like holy hell." He pulled the sling from his trouser pocket and carefully arranged it over his shoulder to support his throbbing wrist and hand.

Maddie laid her head back against the seat cushion and tried to breathe normally, watching the look on the sheriff's face change from furious to surprised to grateful. She wanted to remember the grateful part.

"I have never run that fast in all my life," she said in a breathy voice. "Terribly undignified."

Jericho exhaled a snort of laughter.

But he said not one word for the next half hour. The train swayed around a curve and all at once he fished under the seat for something.

"Hungry?"

"Good heavens, yes. I skipped breakfast."

"Yeah, I noticed." Paper crunched and then he held something out to her. "Biscuit? Probably as cold and hard as saddle leather, but better than listening to your stomach growl all the way to Smoke River."

At once she covered her belly with her hands. "Was it growling, really?"

He gave her one of his raised-eyebrow looks and folded her fingers over a lumpy biscuit. "Eat."

"Right," she murmured. She gobbled it down and held out her hand for another.

The biscuits lasted until Riverton, and during the ten-minute stop she sped into the stationhouse and came back with a cardboard box containing hard-boiled eggs and slices of cold ham. It all disappeared before they rolled through the tiny town of Saint Xavier, and they were still only halfway home.

Maddie found the ball of pink crochet thread and, when her hands stopped shaking, began to work on her lace pattern.

Jericho watched her for a long minute and thought about doing his daily wrist stretches. He settled for right-hand finger flexes. The stuff in Maddie's green bottle had helped, but not enough. He wondered how she'd known what to buy.

After a long silence, she turned toward him with a smile. "We might talk over our next plan," she said happily.

"*We* don't have a plan."

"I have an idea for—"

"Won't wash. The plan is gonna be *my* idea."

She missed a stitch. "Oh? Have you a plan?"

"I might, yeah."

"Jericho…" She folded the length of pink lace

onto her lap. "I apologize for this morning. For making you wait."

"And worry," he added. "And rip my arm half out of its socket." Absently he began to massage his right wrist. "I told myself I shouldn't worry," he said, an edge coming into his voice. "Smart detective lady like you could figure out how to get back to Smoke River. For one thing, you could ride that pretty little mare you're so fond of."

Maddie threw the ball of crochet thread at him. She liked his teasing, she admitted. Up to a point. She liked his eyes and his unkempt dark hair and the strong chin shadowed with a growth of beard. She liked *him*.

Up to a point.

"I want to know what you are thinking, Sheriff."

"No, you don't, Mrs. O'Donnell."

Well, yes, she did. But perhaps now was not the time to push the point. Tomorrow, she decided. After she visited the dressmaker and ordered a new shirtwaist and talked to the bank manager and the Wells Fargo agent again.

After she found out when they planned the next gold shipment.

She let her crochet work drop onto her lap and drew in a deep, clarifying breath. Jericho would insist on his plan, whatever it was. Surely it would be more than sitting on the train, waiting for the Tucker gang to strike? While that had afforded them a good look at the robbers, what they planned next had to result in the capture of at least one of them.

He wouldn't want to include her, but that did not matter.

She had been sent to help Sheriff Jericho Silver, and that is exactly what she intended to do.

Whether he liked it or not.

Chapter Seven

Maddie entered the Smoke River restaurant tired and hungry to find the waitress looking surprisingly pleased to see her. "Evenin', Miss."

"Good evening, Rita. But it's Mrs. O'Donnell. How are you this evening?"

"Feet hurt," the plump woman confessed. "Been on 'em all day, and I worked later than usual knowin' the sheriff would be comin' in for his supper. He eats here most nights, see, and I thought—"

"I thought he would, too," Maddie said. Jericho had bolted off the train the instant it rolled into the station and, without a word, headed off toward the jail. It was obvious he couldn't get away from her fast enough.

Rita led the way to the corner table and Maddie sank onto the upholstered seat.

"Think he'll be along soon?" the waitress ventured. "I saved some of his favorite dessert for him."

"Oh? What is the sheriff's favorite dessert?"

"You won't tell him I told you, will ya, ma'am?

Johnny's mighty fussy about people knowin' personal things about him."

"I will not breathe a word, Rita. I promise."

The waitress leaned down. "Johnny's real partial to peppermint ice cream. Cook makes a good double-layer chocolate cake and the sheriff always has two slices with peppermint ice cream. Maybe you'd like to try some after yer supper?"

Maddie's gaze met the older woman's. "Why do you call the sheriff 'Johnny'? His given name is Jericho, is it not?"

Rita's lined cheeks turned pink. "Well, ma'am, it's 'cuz to some of us the sheriff's special. We've known him since he was a boy, really."

"Oh?" Maddie couldn't help herself; she wanted to know more about the tall, mysterious sheriff. "Oh?" she said again.

Rita smoothed down her starched apron and leaned closer. "Well, ya see, Johnny come to Smoke River when he was just a kid, about twelve years old. He was all alone, never had no family that he knew of. Didn't even know how old he was, really. So we kinda adopted him. Jericho's the name they gave him at the orphanage—from the Bible, you know. Johnny's kind of a pet name the townsfolk gave him."

Johnny. It suited him in a way, Maddie thought. A bit boyish, with a generous dash of what her mother would call "sass." Underneath his taciturn exterior, she suspected there was still a bit of "Johnny."

But when he blustered and swore at her, then he was Jericho for certain—a hard man. A loner who expected the walls to come tumbling down when he made himself known.

She ordered steak with peas and a baked potato, and sat sipping her tea, hoping Jericho—Johnny— would show up. She had some ideas about how to capture the Tucker gang, and besides, she admitted with a little flutter in her chest, the sheriff was certainly the most intriguing man she had ever encountered. It had only been a few hours, but she wanted to see him again. Even his growly voice sent a shiver up her spine.

She consulted the watch pinned to her shirtwaist; another fifteen minutes had passed since the last time she looked and still no sheriff. Apparently he preferred being at the jail to eating supper with her. Part of her felt a bit miffed; another part…well, she wouldn't think about that now, with Rita watching her. She was afraid she would blush.

She sliced up her medium-rare steak with ruthless efficiency, then purposefully mashed down the halved baked potato with her fork and dumped all the butter in the dish on it. While the butter slowly melted, she wondered for the tenth time what the sheriff was doing that was so important he would miss his dinner.

Maddie slowly lowered her fork. Of course. He was off making plans—plans that did not include her. She pressed her lips together. She hated being left out of anything, especially something as important as gold shipments and train robberies and the job she had come to do. An assignment like this made her life worthwhile. And full of adventure. She especially liked the adventure part.

All her life she had felt different somehow. Alone. Even when she was married. She swallowed a little sniffle. Then it had been even worse. Being excluded was her own private version of hell.

Rita slid a piece of cake onto the table and coughed deliberately. Maddie looked up. There he was at the restaurant entrance, tall and long-legged, his smoky eyes scanning the room. She gulped and dug her fork into the butter-drenched potato.

A beaming Rita waved him over and bustled off to bring another menu as the sheriff took the seat across from Maddie.

"You look different," she observed.

His dark eyebrows rose. "Yeah? You mean I look better?"

"Not better, just…different." Her voice came out sharper than usual. In spite of herself, she smarted over his long absence. Now that was just silly. She did not care one fig where Jericho preferred to spend his time.

"Yeah, might be I do look different. Had a shave and got Sandy to trim my hair some. Wearin' a clean shirt might make a difference, too."

It surely did, she admitted. When he was rumpled and unkempt he looked…interesting. All cleaned up, he looked very male and devastatingly handsome. Dangerous, even. For a long minute she could think of nothing to say.

"How about you, Mrs. Detective?"

Maddie bit her lip. "I have enjoyed a bath upstairs in my room, with that nice lavender soap from the mercantile. And," she added with emphasis, "I have almost finished my supper." She did not add *while waiting for you.*

Rita fluttered near with her pad and pencil. "The usual, Johnny?"

"Yep. Well done and—" he glanced at the uneaten peas on Maddie's plate "—skip the peas."

"You do not care for peas?" Maddie blurted out.

"Nope. Can't keep 'em on my knife." He said it with a perfectly straight face, but she laughed anyway.

"And they taste awful when I eat 'em with honey."

She wanted to laugh again, but she did not want to seem the least bit accepting of his humor. Or his late appearance. After all, he had practically stood her up for supper.

She suspected he had been off somewhere making plans, and she itched to know what they were. Besides her duty to the bank manager and Mr. Pinkerton, she did not want to be left out of anything exciting.

Rita brought Jericho's steak and a cup of coffee, and he waited until the waitress retreated to the kitchen before he spoke. "I've been thinking, Maddie. Someone here in Smoke River is tipping off the Tucker gang about the gold shipments. No other way they'd know which train to rob."

Maddie clunked her teacup down on the saucer. "An informer? Who is it?"

"Keep your voice down, dammit."

"Who?" she repeated in a soft murmur.

"Dunno yet. Important thing is to keep my movements secret."

"*Our* movements," Maddie corrected.

"That's what I said." He said it so blithely she was positive he'd said no such thing. And that, she decided, tightening her mouth, was another indication of how he felt about her help on this mission.

She worked to keep her voice calm. "Keep our movements secret, how?"

Jericho swallowed a forkful of fried potatoes. "Set up a smoke screen. Not let anyone see what I'm really doing."

"And just how do *we*—" she purposely emphasized it "—do that? This is a small town. Everybody knows everything that goes on in a town like this."

"You ever camped out in the open overnight?"

"Certainly not. I prefer warmth and privacy and a soft mattress and extra pillows."

"Yeah, I thought so." He grinned and munched up a bite of steak. "Fact is, I'm betting you'd rather hightail it back to the city than sleep on the hard ground."

Maddie put down her fork. "Not if I could capture some train robbers. In that case I would endure anything. Well, almost anything. Not bugs or wolves or thunderstorms."

His smoke-blue eyes regarded her for a full minute. "Let's face it, Maddie. You're too citified for my plan."

Maddie opened her mouth, then snapped it shut until the impulse to scream passed. "For a good cause, I can be so uncitified you would not recognize me."

"Uh-huh."

He didn't believe her. "Jericho, what *is* your plan? Tell me."

He swigged down the last of his coffee and sank his fork into the slab of chocolate cake Rita had brought. It was twice the size of Maddie's piece. Oh, yes, this man certainly was "Johnny" to those who knew him well. And, she thought with growing respect, those who knew him well, loved him.

But that most definitely did not include her.

Jericho swallowed a mouthful of cake. "I'm going after the gang tomorrow morning. Alone."

"Not without me," Maddie retorted sharply. "You underestimate me, Sheriff, and I will not stand for it. I am carrying out an assignment for Mr. Pinkerton and you cannot —"

"Shut up, Maddie. Just shut the hell up, will you? I can do whatever the hell I want."

She went as white as flour. A tension so thick you could cut it like an overdone steak dropped over the room. Maddie stared at him.

"I don't want you along," he said, his voice quiet.

She pressed her lips together. "I came out here to help you catch the Tucker gang," she said, in an equally quiet voice. "And until you can shoot straight with both your hands, you are stuck with me."

Jericho made up his mind for the third time. He sure as hell wasn't stuck with her. She wasn't used to the West. She always slept indoors, on a soft mattress; she didn't like bugs. She'd never be able to manage what he had in mind. He knew it, but she didn't, at least not yet. The woman was so damn stubborn....

Jumping jennies, how could he get her out of his hair? *And his mind.*

He sucked in a quick gulp of air. He wished to hell she'd just climb on the train back to Chicago where she belonged, and he wished she'd do it now, before she got hurt.

He didn't like his reaction to her. Something about her sure set his teeth on edge. He found himself uneasy and tense when she was around.

"Listen, Maddie. Today I sat down with Colonel Wash Halliday and studied an army map. If I'm figuring it right, I know where the gang will try next. I've got an idea where they'll hole up and I'm going to surprise them before they stop the train."

"But—"

"You're a good sport, Maddie, but you've grown up soft and citified. Forget it. You're not coming with me."

"You are wasting your breath, Jericho. I took this job and I intend to finish it."

"Oh, no, you won't," he growled. One thing he was learning about Mrs. Detective—she had enough sand to try anything. What she didn't have was good sense.

She looked him straight in the eye. "Don't argue, Sheriff. We've been through this before, but apparently you are hard of hearing because—" she raised her voice until she was shouting "—whatever you plan on doing, *I am doing it with you!*"

They stared at each other in silence. He respected her dedication. He admired her grit. But this pretty lady was just too much pretty lady to be any real help. She distracted him, and besides, he preferred to work alone; he always had. He wasn't about to change for Madison O'Donnell.

She had sand, all right, but she wouldn't last an hour on the trail with him. He knew it, but she didn't.

He admired her can-do attitude. What he didn't like was his reaction to her. He was scared of something. Not her, exactly. But something about her sure set his teeth on edge.

Chapter Eight

Jericho reined up and sat listening to the morning sounds that were beginning to turn night into day—the squawk of a jay, doves burbling under mesquite bushes. The light was turning from gray to peach and the hills ahead were tinged with pink.

But it was another sound that stopped him. Someone was following him. Had been for the last ten miles or so. Whoever it was wasn't subtle about it, so he knew he wasn't being stalked; if he were, the rider would stop when he stopped and move on only when he did.

Maybe an Indian? No. He'd never hear an Indian until too late, and anyway most of the tribes knew him on sight and wouldn't care what he was up to. He lifted the reins and moved on.

When he reached a copse of alders, he dismounted, made sure his horse was hidden, unsheathed his rifle and waited.

Within half an hour a mare he recognized drew into his sights and he swore under his breath. A young cowboy plodded toward him on Sandy's horse. It wasn't Sandy, so who the hell…?

Jericho stepped into his path and raised the rifle. "Hold it right there, mister. Hands in the air."

The rider—a boy, he gathered from the size of his small frame—froze and looked up.

Maddie. Damn it to hell. He took one look at her, her body drooping over the neck of the horse and swore again. "Hot damn in a haystack!"

What had happened to Mrs. Mint-Ice-Cream Detective? She looked like a lost orphan, and he winced at the needle of pain in his chest. He must have looked just like that once.

The shirt hung off her shoulders, though it sure buttoned up nice over the swell of her breasts. She'd rolled up her jeans at the bottom, but they fit just right everywhere else. The boots—oh, hell, he recognized Sandy's boots. They were four sizes too big. Her toes were probably wriggling around in nothing but air. How had she talked Sandy out of them?

She looked like a half-grown boy dressed up like his pa.

She needed a neckerchief. And her hat, damnation! Somewhere she'd found a small-size black Stetson that looked stylish over her pinned-up hair. Too stylish.

"What the devil are you doing out here?"

"Following you. Or trying to. I am not experienced at tracking."

"Go home, Maddie. Turn your horse around and skedaddle back to town."

She just looked at him.

"You hear me?"

She nodded but didn't move an inch.

"I don't want you, Mrs. Detective. Get it through your thick head, will ya? *I don't want you.*"

"I know," she said, her voice quiet. "But you need me, just the same. And I am here now, so why do you not just be quiet and get on with whatever it is *we* are going to do?"

"I ought to—oh, the hell with it." Maddie O'Donnell was like a dollop of pitch; once it stuck to your fingers, no matter what you did, it was still there, being sticky. Too late to talk her out of anything, he figured. Besides, they were too far out to send her back now; within an hour she'd be lost.

"I never give up, Sheriff."

"Yeah. I guess I knew that." Dammit, anyway.

He unbuckled his leather belt, yanked the blue bandanna from his neck and handed them over. "Hand over your hat."

"My hat? What for? It fits perfectly."

"It's too fancy." He snatched it off her head, dropped it onto the ground and stomped on it a half dozen times. She watched him, her face flushed and growing stiffer every minute. He handed the Stetson back to her, noting with satisfaction that the feather in the band was bedraggled and bent in two places.

"Thank. You. Very. Much." Her voice was glacial.

"Had to get the 'new' out. Same with your duds." He looked meaningfully at her shirt and jeans. She clapped both arms across her body. "Oh, no, you don't."

Jericho stepped in close, dragged her out of the saddle and dropped her in the dirt. Then he knelt over her and with his left hand pushed her down flat and rolled her over and over until her garments looked dusty and wrinkled. It made his right wrist hurt like hell, but it couldn't be helped. She had to look scruffier.

When he was finished she looked mad enough to spit bullets. He snaked his belt through the loops at her waist and tightened the leather with a jerk while she glared at him.

He looked her over. "Nope, too tight," he observed. "Gives you too much of a waistline." *And a hipline. And a bustline.*

He loosened the belt until her jeans hung loose around her hips and knotted the bandanna around her neck. Patting her dark mare he noted the saddlebag she carried. Probably full of undergarments.

"Remount," he ordered.

She hesitated. "I do not think—"

"Either mount up or shut up."

Her head jerked up. "You are despicable."

"You are damned difficult. Makes us even."

In cold silence he made a step out of his laced fingers and shoved her up into the saddle. Gritting his teeth against the pain, he climbed onto Dancer and reined away.

"Follow me."

"Damn right," she muttered under her breath.

Those were the last words she said for the next ten miles. He didn't expect her to last more than a couple more hours, but she surprised him.

He tried to ignore the tense silence between them. When the sun arced overhead and the green-and-gold countryside stretched before them he tried to focus on the scenery instead of the set look on her face. Her eyes were so turbulent they made him think of green stones heated in a campfire. Pines and fir trees so green they looked black, blue chicory blossoms, and scarlet paintbrush helped keep his mind off her.

There was no trail. Jericho headed cross-country without slowing his pace or changing direction.

Or stopping to rest, Maddie noted. He was like a well-oiled machine that never faltered. And she was most certainly not well oiled. Her joints were beginning to ache like an old woman's and her throat was so dry and dusty she could not even spit.

At last, Jericho raised one hand and halted near a copse of cottonwoods by a spring. He slipped off his mount, led her horse to water and waited for her to dismount.

She tried it. "I cannot lift my leg that high."

"Lift your leg frontways, up over the saddle horn."

She gritted her teeth. "I—I cannot."

His voice hardened. "Then bump your butt off backwards over the saddle lip and slide off the mare's rump."

"I can't let go of the reins," she muttered. "My fingers are cramped in place."

Jericho stomped toward her, pulled off one leather riding glove and laid his warm hand over hers. Then he kneaded the joints until she could loosen her grip.

"Oh," she moaned. "Ouch. Oh, this is simply awful."

He shot her a look but said nothing.

She managed to let go of the reins and shift her body toward him. Keeping his injured arm at his side, he extended his left hand up to her. "Okay, now slide off."

He reached to steady her, but when her feet hit the ground, her knees buckled and her body slammed against his.

He felt hard, hot and damp with sweat, but thank goodness he was there. He smelled of leather and horse and sweat and something pepperminty. His breath? She swallowed and wondered what she smelled like to him—certainly not lavender after miles of choking dust and perspiration.

He stuck a canvas-covered metal canteen in her hand and led her mare off to the spring. She gulped a mouthful of the metallic-tasting water. "How much farther?" she gasped.

"About fourteen miles."

She groaned and gulped down more water. "I cannot ride fourteen more miles."

"Yeah, you damn well can. You wanted this. Besides, I'm betting you're stronger than you look."

"You would lose, Sheriff. I am what you see before you."

Jericho studied her with weary eyes. "I see a

tired, stubborn city girl who wishes she'd never left Chicago."

She didn't answer. She hadn't breath enough to argue.

"You'll feel better when we make camp and you can soak your muscles in a cold stream."

"When will that be?"

"Four, maybe five hours. Maybe a little more."

"Would it be less if we rode faster?"

"Might, but that wouldn't be smart. Don't want to raise a lot of dust that could be seen."

"By the Tucker gang? Where do you think they are?"

"Dunno for sure. Could be anywhere. Come on, time to mount up."

Maddie gritted her teeth. Maybe Jericho was right. The West was rough and unforgiving for a woman. If she lived through this, she would never, never leave the city again.

After another grueling three hours, she lost track of time. The pine trees merged into larch and cottonwood groves, the vegetation grew more and more sparse. Patches of buttercups spotted the ground, along with an occasional knee-high bush with prickly stems and pale pink flowers.

The dry air parched her throat; it smelled of sage and something else—wood smoke, maybe. The scent reminded her of food and her stomach began to growl so continuously she was sure Jericho could hear it.

Not once did he twist in his saddle to check on

her and he never slowed his pace, just kept moving steadily forward in front of her. Fatigue made her tilt to one side. She righted herself with a jerk, only to find herself gradually leaning to the other side.

Fighting to prevent her eyelids from drooping shut, she started to sing to keep up her spirits. "She was only a girl from the country, you see…"

"Hush up!" Jericho ordered. He rode back to her side. "A voice carries out here."

"Are we close to anything important?"

"Might be. Can't be sure." He pulled ahead of her and as he passed she heard him murmur, "Don't drop behind. Stay close."

Her nerves froze. He knew something. Or sensed something. She tried to keep up, but little by little she lagged behind him. The blazing late-afternoon sun that had blinded her all day ebbed into a gloomy, gray dusk and then blackened into night.

She had never been outside in such total darkness. In Chicago, all the streets and storefronts were lighted. Here, trees became men with clutching arms; shrubs loomed like crouching animals. Maddie shivered, but not from cold. She would never admit it, but she was frightened.

"Jericho?" she called softly.

"Just ahead another mile or two," he intoned. "Good camping place."

Thank goodness. That meant supper and a chance to wash the dust and perspiration from her sticky skin. And sleep!

He drew rein beside a haphazard pile of river rocks

bordering a shallow creek. While she struggled to get down off her horse, he dismounted and tramped off into the dark, apparently to make sure the place was safe. The mere thought sent a chill up the back of her neck.

By the time he stalked back to her mare, she had managed to slide off the horse's back, but again her legs gave way. This time she grabbed on to the horse's bushy tail and stood shaking with exhaustion until Jericho approached.

Without a word he reached out his good hand and pulled her upright. "Can you walk?"

She tried a step and tottered. "No. My legs do not do what I tell them."

He frog-marched her to the stream and plopped her down on the sandy bank. "Roll up your jeans and get your legs in the water. It'll be cold, but try to stay there as long as you can."

Jericho left her hunched over, her limbs submerged in the creek and her neck bent so far her chin almost touched her shirtfront. For damn sure she wasn't cut out for this. He'd wanted to teach her a lesson, but he didn't want her to die on the trail.

With a snort he turned his thoughts to supper, dug a small hole in the ground and built a fire. It burned hot and made no smoke.

Maddie stumbled back to camp, her jeans soaked up to her crotch and her cheeks dewy with water she'd splashed over her face and neck.

"Sit," he ordered.

She sank down where she stood.

"Closer to the fire. If you want to dry out quicker, take off your trousers and hang them on a bush."

"I most certainly will not." Her voice sounded so forlorn he felt a little jab of regret. For a woman who hadn't ridden much, she had done surprisingly well.

On the other hand, he told himself, she'd asked for it. Begged for it, in fact. But when he saw how tough this was for her, something inside him began to soften.

The summer night was mild, with a thin silver crescent of a moon. He liked nights like this: not enough light to be seen and not cold enough to bundle up. Nights like this at the orphanage he'd sneak out to sleep in the corn patch.

He searched in his saddlebags for a can of beans, some of the dried jerky he always carried and a can of fancy apricots. The beans he pried open with his pocketknife and set in the fire.

When the tin was black and the beans steaming, he offered Maddie the spoon. "Careful, they're hot."

She gobbled three heaping spoonfuls and stopped. "Why aren't you eating?"

"Only got one spoon," he said.

Instantly she held the utensil out to him. "Then we will share."

He was too hungry to argue. She'd probably think it unsanitary, but at least she was eating. He noticed that each time she handed the spoon back, her fingers shook. His breath hitched in.

They ate out of the single can until the spoon

scraped bottom. To his surprise, Maddie said very little.

They ate the apricots the same way. Each time Jericho glanced at her he felt a twinge of concern and a healthy dose of apprehension.

By the time he untied the blankets rolled up behind his saddle and spread them out by the fire, his belly was doing flips.

The last thing he wanted to do was to like this woman, but he couldn't help admitting she was a courageous companion, capable of strength he'd never thought possible. Also, when she kept quiet, she wasn't bad company.

But it was crazy to bring her out into the wilderness where he had nothing to do but listen to that whiskey-burred voice and watch those damn green eyes widen at all the things she wasn't used to, the cry of an owl, a coyote yelping on the next ridge, even the whiffle and stomp of the horses picketed a few yards away.

He strode off to the stream to wash the spoon. When he returned she was eyeing the two side-by-side bedrolls. She bent down to grab one corner of the closest blanket, then straightened with a groan and looked at him.

"Must they be so close together?"

Jericho lifted his hands, palms up. "Not safe to be separated, Maddie. Sorry, city lady, I don't have any fancy pillows."

She sent him a look that made his heart do a somersault. "I can manage without pillows," she said tightly. "What I cannot abide is…is…" Her voice cracked.

Jericho sighed. "Is sleeping next to me."

"Well, yes, but it is more than that. It's being left in the dark, not knowing what you are planning. I like to be part of things on an assignment."

"What you mean is you like to run things your way. Out here—" he waved his good hand at their camp "—you're out of your depth."

"You mean," she said in a weary voice, "that out here I am helpless."

He could practically see the bristles popping up along her spine. Her lips trembled, but she forced them into an unsmiling line.

"I admit I feel off-balance out here in the middle of nowhere, Jericho. But I am here, whether you like it or not. And whatever your—*our*—plan is, I intend to help."

Something inside planted a hand on his heart. Damn her dogged, single-minded sense of duty. He worried about the burden she'd be out here. She knew nothing about this country. He'd have to nursemaid her every step of the way, protect her from snakes, saddle sores, scratchy bedrolls, spiders and other dangers, including the Tucker gang.

The last thing he'd wanted was to get roped into protecting her; made him nervous being responsible for anyone other than himself. Especially a woman.

Especially *this* woman. Mrs. Detective couldn't keep her pretty little nose out of anything and she paid no attention to her own limitations. She could get herself hurt or even killed. That thought pumped cold, sweaty fear into his gut.

This whole thing was making him crazy.

"Jericho?"

Her measured voice sounded an alarm in the back of his brain. "Yeah?"

"I do not believe I can sleep like this." She pointed to the two side-by-side bedrolls.

"You got another idea?"

She said nothing, just snapped her mouth closed. He kicked dirt over the fire, hobbled both horses, and sat down on one of the blankets.

"Get some shut-eye, Mrs. Detective. Tomorrow could be rough."

He slipped the sling off his injured arm, forced himself to do a dozen wrist stretches and deliberately flexed each of the fingers of his right hand. It hurt too much to do more. He grabbed the bottle of painkiller, swallowed a double mouthful and shucked his boots. Folding them up with his Colt underneath, he laid them under his head. Then he positioned the two rifles he'd brought next to him and patted the bedroll beside his.

"Come on, Maddie, crawl in. You've got to get some sleep."

Maddie glowered at him. He wanted her to wrap herself up like a sausage in a smelly old blanket? He made it look easy, but… Oh, all right, she would try it.

She planted her bottom on the wool and let out a cry. Her derriere was on fire! Quickly she scooched down to a prone position, kicked off Sandy's huge boots and folded the blanket edges over her body.

"Good girl," the motionless figure beside her murmured.

Tears threatened, but she blinked them back. Even if every inch of her ached as if she had rolled down Mt. Everest, and even if she felt like having a good cry, she felt absurdly pleased with herself. Tomorrow, she vowed, she would do even better. Jericho would be proud of her.

A hard knot formed in her belly. *Careful, Maddie. Do not look to this man for approval. Do not let him become important.* Beyond showing her how to survive in this wild country, Sheriff Jericho Silver had nothing she wanted.

Nothing.

She had learned her lesson the hard way. Trapped in a suffocating marriage when she was too young to know better, the life in her had been all but snuffed out. She would never, never let that happen again.

Chapter Nine

Jericho laid his arm across Maddie's slumbering form and put his mouth so close to her ear he could smell her lavender scent. "Don't move," he murmured. "And don't make a sound. Someone's coming."

Maddie snapped her eyes open to a star-dotted sky and an impenetrable thick blackness surrounding them. She had not been asleep, but she had heard nothing in the quiet but the shuffling of the horses and the occasional *tu-whoo* of an owl.

What was it Jericho heard? She tipped her head sideways until her lips brushed the rim of his ear. "I hear nothing," she whispered.

Jericho did not answer. Very slowly he slid his Colt from under his boots. He didn't cock it—the click would be audible. Instead, he rested the barrel on the slight rise his knee made under the blanket, aimed it across the cold fire pit and waited.

There it was again, a soft step and the breathing

of a third person. Maddie froze and he could tell she was trying not to breathe.

A twig cracked somewhere behind the horses and Jericho adjusted his aim. Whoever it was halted. Maddie gripped his arm and he winced.

The silence stretched. He felt the gentle gust of Maddie's exhaled air curl into the shell of his ear and his controlled breathing grew unsteady.

Jesus and Joseph, now was not the time to get hot and bothered by a woman; he had to concentrate. He peered into the darkness but could see nothing. Then came a tiny sound, like something rubbing against a smooth surface.

At once he knew who was out there. He lay back down and slid the Colt back under his boots. Maddie again clutched his sore arm and without thinking he brushed her hand away. He heard her soft gasp. He leaned over her and once more brought his mouth to her ear.

"Relax, Maddie. I know who it is. He won't harm us."

She tilted her face up to his. "How do you know that?" she whispered.

He laid his hand over her rigid form. "Just lie still. I'll explain later."

They waited. Jericho kept his gaze on the horses; they moved restlessly but didn't slip the hobbles. Beside him, Maddie began to tremble. He wanted to say something to calm her, but he'd have to wait until the intruder was gone.

It wasn't so bad, lying here next to her. It had been

a long time since he'd been this close to a woman. He'd forgotten how good they smelled.

At last he heard quiet footfalls moving away from their camp and then the far-off nicker of a pony. He waited five more minutes, then lifted his hand off Maddie and sat up.

"He's gone," he said, keeping his voice low.

"Who is gone? Who was it?"

Jericho chuckled softly. "An old Indian brave, Nez Percé, I'd guess. Every damn time I'm on the trail he sneaks up at night and searches my saddlebags."

"What does he want?"

"Food. We ran his tribe off their land, and now they're starving. I always leave a little jerky and some biscuits or something for him to find. Gotten kinda used to it. One of these nights I'm gonna surprise him with a chocolate cake."

She drew herself up to a sitting position beside him. "I feel sorry for someone who does not have enough to eat. I hardly know what to say."

Jericho barked out a laugh. "Well, that's a first." He settled back on his blanket and stared up at the ceiling of stars overhead. It was nice when she blew her breath into his ear. Real nice. Made him tingle all over.

Maddie woke when the sun turned the sky to gold and heated her body through the blanket. She yawned and rolled over to look at Jericho.

He was gone! Heavens, surely he would not abandon her in this wild, uncivilized place? Her hands closed into tight fists. When she saw him again—if she ever did—she would grab her pistol and shoot him right between those maddening blue eyes. She patted the small firearm she carried in her jeans pocket.

But she couldn't just lie here thinking murderous thoughts. She bolted upright, shook out her bedroll and folded it up with hands that trembled. Oh, goodness, every muscle in her body was so sore she could scarcely move. Groaning, she pulled on Sandy's huge leather boots and limped through the brush down to the creek.

There he was, kneeling on a flat rock scooping water over his face, neck and bare chest. So he hadn't abandoned her! Relief made her a bit giddy. Without a word she settled a few feet upstream and began washing her face.

"I thought you had left me alone out here," she said between splashes.

He looked at her as if she were painted purple. "You crazy? You'd survive out here about twenty-four hours and I'd hang for murder."

"That is certainly an excellent reason for not riding off." She used her best put-him-in-his-place voice.

Jericho hurriedly dried his face and chest with his shirt and shrugged into it. "I wouldn't ride off and leave you, Maddie. Lord knows I might *want* to, but I wouldn't."

"Are you sure?"

He eyed her with some disgust. "You have my word on it."

"I find it hard to believe you."

He marched up close enough to spit at her. "Out here in the West there's two things you can always believe in, Mrs. Back-East-Detective. A man's word and a man's handshake."

Maddie stood up and faced him. "Jericho Silver, if you lie to me you will live to regret it."

"Oh, for—I haven't lied, and I'm already living to regret it. You don't have much faith in people, do you?"

"No, I do not."

He buttoned his damp shirt. "Is it all men you don't trust, or just me?"

"All men," she said pointedly. "In my line of work, most of the men I come in contact with are criminals on the run. The rest of them just want to chain you up in a pumpkin shell."

"Huh?"

"You know," she said in exasperation. "Men want to marry you. Lock you up in a prison."

"Well, dammit, here's one man who doesn't. I just want to get you back to Chicago in one piece. As soon as possible," he added.

Her face changed. "Are we going back to Smoke River today?"

"Nope. We're gonna do what I we—*I*—set out to do—find the Tucker gang."

She marched to her mare, and he watched with interest when she grabbed her left foot with both hands and lifted it toward the stirrup. Finally she gave up, grabbed for the saddle horn, and awkwardly pulled herself on top of the horse, belly down.

But she'd forgotten to tighten the cinch. She straightened and urged the mare forward maybe six paces and the saddle slipped sideways off the mare's back and dumped her onto the ground.

"Unpack your saddlebag," he ordered. He pointed to where it was haphazardly slung behind the saddle. "Pack it so it's balanced on both sides. A horse doesn't cotton to an uneven load."

Maddie groaned. He was giving orders like an army sergeant.

He urged his mount forward, then pulled up. "And don't use any more of that lavender soap in the morning."

"But I always wash my—"

"Don't," he interrupted. "I think one of the outlaws might be Sioux. Indian," he clarified for her. "An Indian can smell a campfire, or a smelly woman, a mile away."

"Smelly!"

"Perfumy," he amended. "Don't use any scent or powder."

Maddie's jaw muscles tightened until they ached. Orders, orders and more orders. Did the man never say "please"?

Jericho reined closer and peered into her face. "You okay? You look kinda funny."

"No, I am not okay! I am so tired my eyelids feel stuck together, and I am sick of taking orders."

"Tough. You wanted to come along on this jaunt, so now you take orders."

"Aye-aye, Captain," she shot. "I would salute, but I am so tired I cannot lift my arm."

A low chuckle rumbled in his throat. "Try it, anyway."

Just to spite him, she snapped a salute. This time he laughed outright.

She liked it when he laughed. His eyes got all twinkly and so deep and clear blue she could drown in their depths.

"All right, Mrs. Detective." He touched two fingers to his hat brim. "Try to keep close. In an hour, you'll see a big sugar pine scorched by lightning on one side. We'll rest there."

He was gone before she could think of something provocative to say. Well, not provocative, exactly; she disliked women who flirted. Just something that would make him laugh again.

She looked mad enough to chew nails. Without a word he walked his horse past her. "And Maddie, don't forget to tighten that wide band underneath the horse's belly. It's called a cinch. It's what keeps the saddle on."

The sound of his horse faded. Good. He was out of her hair and she could relax.

But she couldn't. She managed to remount using the belly-down-on-the-saddle method, and she rode for what seemed like hours thinking about Jericho's smoky eyes and that lopsided smile she rarely saw. What a puzzle of a man the sheriff was.

An hour later she spied the blackened tree, and there he was, sitting under it in a patch of straggly green-looking weeds with little star-shaped flowers. She slid off the horse, winced and plopped down next to him. "Ow. Ouch!"

He uncrossed his long legs. "Still sore, huh?"

"Yes," she said.

"Not surprising. A rider as green as you are might not move at all after twenty miles in the saddle."

She glared at him while he sliced a piece from a strip of dried jerky and handed them over balanced on the blade of his pocketknife.

Maddie peered at it. "What is that?"

"Jerky. Dried venison. Smoked it myself in a shack I built out in back of the jail."

She picked up a single piece and sniffed at it. "Smells like smoked ham." She popped it past her lips.

"Don't chew it right away," Jericho cautioned. "Just hold it in your mouth till it softens up some."

"Ow rong?" Her words came out garbled with the meat still in her mouth. "I am bery hunglee."

He'd just opened his mouth to answer when he spotted something over her shoulder.

"Why aroo starling at me?"

He pointed his forefinger behind her. "Smoke."

She swallowed suddenly, choked, and began to cough. "Smoke?"

"Told ya to let that soften some."

"Smoke?" she repeated. She twisted to look behind her.

"See it?" he said. "Must be a camp over yonder."

Maddie struggled to her feet. "Aren't we going to investigate? What if it's the Tucker gang?"

"I'm pretty sure it *is* the Tucker gang. That bein' the case, why would I want to investigate in broad daylight? Sit down, Maddie. We'll wait till sundown."

She looked at him for a long time, then sank down beside him and snatched the other piece of jerky off his knife blade. Good, he thought. Chewing on it would keep her quiet and give him some time to think.

"Jericho, it is probably only—" she glanced up at the orange ball of sun overhead "—nine o'clock in the morning. What are we going to do until dark?"

"Don't know about you," he said slowly. "Me, I'm just gonna relax, maybe play some mumblety-peg."

A frown wrinkled her forehead. "Play— How can you do that when outlaws are around?"

He sliced off another round of jerky. "Nuthin' else to do till the sun goes down, that's why. People out here in the West get used to waiting."

She folded her hands, then refolded them and finally stuffed them in her jean pockets. "Mumblety-whatever-it-is is all very well for you, but what am *I* going to do?"

He studied her. This morning her eyes were sea-green and troubled. Funny, he never noticed before how thick her lashes were. "You don't like to spend time doin' nothing, huh?"

She looked startled. "No, I do not. It reminds me of when I was married."

Again he found his brows rising. "Odd way to look at bein' married. Seems to me there'd be lots of things to do if you were married." Lots and lots of things.

Her gaze narrowed and he shut off that line of thinking. "How 'bout I teach you to play mumblety-peg?"

The soft-looking mouth firmed into a hard line. "I do not think so, Sheriff. That is a skill I would never use in Chicago."

"Suit yourself."

"I will indeed."

She was quiet for exactly thirty seconds. "Is there more jerky?"

Jericho cut two more pieces of dried venison. He kept slicing and she kept eating for maybe an hour; then she began to fidget like a hen with a fox on the prowl.

Hell, let her fidget. Teach her a lesson about catching criminals out West, which she obviously knew nothing about. Which is why he hadn't wanted her along in the first place.

He stretched out on a grassy patch and covered his face with his hat. Under the wide brim, he surreptitiously watched her pace around and around the horses. She made the circuit maybe twenty times, then circled the sugar pine for so many revolutions he expected her to get dizzy and stagger off into the copse of cottonwoods.

Then she started practicing some kind of dance steps, whirling around and around with her arms stretched out. Waltzing, he guessed. He'd tried it once or twice. Couldn't imagine doing it with Maddie. Just thinking about holding her in his arms made him sweat.

After the dance steps she skipped rocks into the river and sang songs to herself under her breath. *"Oh, Columbia, the gem of the ocean..."*

Skip-plop.

"Blow high! Blow low! A-sailing down the coasts of High Barbary..."

Skip-skip-plop.

"She was a proper lady, and he a one-eyed jack..."

That one caught Jericho's interest. "Where'd you learn that?"

She broke off the tune. "From my father," she said with a blush. "He used to come home from the bank inebriated in the afternoon, and he would sing such songs just to shock my mother."

Interesting parents, he thought. But at least she *had* parents. He sure couldn't see Maddie as a young girl in an orphanage.

She went on singing and he drifted off to sleep, thinking about a woman who'd get riled up by nothing but a song. He guessed big-city women were touchy about some things.

When he woke, Maddie was perched beside him, her knees propped up, her chin in her hands. Bored to death, he figured. He fished for his pocketknife. "Come on, I'll show you how to play mumblety-peg."

She grasped the game in just one round, and after that he found it a challenge to beat her. Her delicate-looking hands were stronger than they looked and her coordination was good. Better than good. He'd like to challenge her to a shooting match, but it'd make too much noise. She'd already proved she was a crack shot with a pistol. How would she handle a rifle? He glanced at the two Winchesters secured in their long scabbards tied onto his saddle.

"Jericho," she accused, "you are not paying attention."

"You're right, I'm not. I'm wondering some things about you."

She looked up. "Oh? What things? I wonder things about you, as well."

He wasn't sure he wanted to pursue this conversation, wasn't sure he wanted her to know what was on his mind. But he'd sure like to know what was on hers.

Or maybe he didn't. She was probably still mad about that twenty miles they'd ridden yesterday. Even though she'd halfway impressed him by keeping up, she was still a greenhorn.

"Why did you want to be sheriff of a small town like Smoke River?" She kept her eyes on his face.

"Guess I want to keep law and order, same as most sheriffs."

"Does it have anything to do with that Indian girl at the orphanage?"

Jericho swallowed. "Yeah, kinda." He looked off at the purple-gray mountains to the east. "I don't like injustice. This is a wild country and sometimes people do wild things."

She nodded in understanding and he presented his own question. "Why did you want to be a Pinkerton agent?"

Unexpectedly, she laughed. "Same as you, Sheriff. I like catching criminals. I like the challenge."

"Huh. Maybe we're both crazy."

"I do not think that is crazy, Jericho. Perhaps we are doing different things but for the same reason. You are the sheriff of Smoke River, and I am a Pinkerton agent. Both of us want to find something of value in life."

A thread of unease tickled the back of his neck. "Yeah? What kind of 'something'?"

"Something that…matters," she said slowly. "Something that is worth doing, not just for oneself but for people around us."

For a moment he couldn't speak over the hunk of granite stuck in his throat. "Maybe." His palms began to sweat. "Most women would find that in their husband. Or their children. That's something they care about beyond themselves."

"Ye-es, perhaps." She looked up into his eyes and his throat closed again. She'd touched on something he'd hungered for all his life, having a family. It scared the hell out of him. Yeah, he was hungry. But he'd never again risk caring about someone.

Their gazes locked and his heartbeat kicked up a notch. Two notches. He fought the urge to run for his horse and gallop as far away from her as he could get.

"It would seem that we are somewhat alike," she said, still holding his eyes. "Imagine that, a light-hearted eastern city lady and a serious, upright Western sheriff finding themselves working on the same side."

He busied himself folding up his jackknife. "You're not light-hearted, Maddie. You're lying to yourself if you think you are."

"I never lie to myself," she said calmly. "But you know something, Jericho? I think you do."

Dumbstruck, he stared at her. It was as though she'd peeked under his skin and seen what he'd wrestled with all these years. Seen the hunger for a home, a family, like other men; seen that hunger stunted for fear of losing it.

He stood up suddenly and strode to his horse. With jerky motions he tightened the cinch and mounted up.

"Time to stop jawing and move on, Mrs. Detective."

Chapter Ten

Jericho touched his heels to Dancer's side. "Let's move."

"But it is not yet sundown," Maddie protested.

"It will be by the time we get where we're going. Mount up."

"But—"

He picked up his pace. "Don't argue, dammit. I know what I'm doing."

Maddie blinked at his hostile tone. "Yes, sir, Mr. Sheriff. Sir." She thought about saluting again, but he was facing away from her. "Maddening man," she muttered under her breath.

But of course he *did* know what he was doing, even if he was not polite about it. Without him, she would be completely helpless out here in this wild, uncivilized country.

She fumbled beneath the horse's belly and jerked the cinch tight as he had instructed. The mare gave a sharp whinny and sidled away from her. She ignored Jericho's laugh and tried to heave herself into the saddle.

After three attempts she managed to stuff her foot into the stirrup and swing up onto the horse's broad back. Out of breath with the effort, she looped the reins around one hand and kicked the animal hard.

The mare jolted forward. Maddie grabbed on to the saddle horn just as Jericho twisted around to see what was keeping her. Instantly she released her grip and straightened in the saddle. As nonchalantly as she could manage, she walked the horse abreast of his.

"Since we are riding together on this mission," she began, carefully modulating her voice into her Excruciatingly Polite tone, "would you care to tell me what your—*our*—plan is?"

"I'll tell you when we get there. Follow me and don't talk. If," he added with dry emphasis, "you can manage it."

He trotted his mount off and did not once turn back to check on her. She'd done something to anger him. Again. And she racked her brain to figure out what it was this time.

Perhaps he was simply being a man, always wanting to be in charge. Wanting no responsibility for anyone but himself.

With sudden clarity she knew that was the key. He had cared about that Indian girl at the orphanage, and when she died from the whipping, Jericho felt responsible. Worse, he felt guilty for not speaking up for her. And now he was afraid to take responsibility for someone or to risk caring for someone ever again.

And that, she deduced in a sudden moment of clarity, was why Sheriff Silver preferred to work alone. The man wanted to risk no one's life but his own.

Furthermore, she was beginning to understand, Jericho had shut himself off from life to protect himself.

But he was wrong.

Hours later they walked their horses to the top of a lumpy, weed-covered hill, dismounted quietly and peered down through a screen of larch and scrub pine trees.

Below them a camp was laid out, tucked into a ragged circle of gray boulders near the river. A fire pit puffed smoke into the air, which added to the shadowy gloom as the sun slipped behind the mountains to the west.

"I figure that's Tucker's camp," Jericho said quietly. "We're about five miles from the Oregon Central railroad tracks. For a gang of train robbers, that's within striking distance."

Maddie sat on her horse without saying a word, and for once, he wished she'd say something. With a sigh, he began to calculate how long it would take for dusk to fade into darkness.

"We've got about twenty minutes," he said quietly.

"Twenty minutes for what?"

"Full dark."

"And then what? It would help if you would tell me what the plan is, Jericho."

His plan. His plan was what it always was when he tracked a man, or a gang. It had always worked. He bluffed them into believing they were outnumbered and that he was just one of many armed lawmen. By the time they realized he was alone, it was too late. He was good at capturing outlaws, and he always, *always* worked alone.

But, dammit, this time was different. He prayed the result would be the same—he'd capture every one of them.

"When it gets dark, here's what I want you to do." He didn't look at her. He didn't want to see the questioning look on her face, but he knew it was there. He slipped both Winchesters out of the saddle scabbards and gestured ahead.

"I want you to take one of my rifles and crawl down behind those boulders."

Maddie sucked in her breath but said nothing.

"Stick your hat on a branch and prop it up so it shows above a different boulder, about ten feet away. Got that?"

"Got it," she murmured. She sounded surprisingly calm.

"I'm gonna fire one bullet into the camp. When you hear a second shot, you start yelling like crazy and jiggle your hat up and down. Fire your rifle, then crawl to cover and keep firing."

"Keep firing," she echoed.

"You do know how to shoot a rifle, don't you?" Hell and damn, he should have asked that before.

"I can shoot anything with bullets in it," she answered tightly. "Even a Sharps buffalo gun."

Jericho shot a look at her face. Just as well he couldn't see her clearly. No matter what fearless expression she adopted, he wouldn't believe it. He prayed she wasn't lying about the rifle.

He leaned toward her. "You ready?"

"I am most certainly ready."

He almost laughed aloud. Maddie was one helluva good bluffer. "Okay, then. Go!"

She hoisted the rifle across her folded arms, crouched low, and disappeared down the hill. Nothing happened for a quarter of an hour, and Jericho began to sweat. She'd bullied her way into this mess, but God knew he didn't want her to pay for it with her life.

He settled his own hat on a pine branch and waited five more long minutes until he saw her dark Stetson poke up from a rocky crevice. He belly-crawled to a stand of coyote bush, thumbed off the safety on his rifle, and fired one shot into the campfire below.

Five men scrambled for cover.

Jericho lifted his head. "Tucker?" he shouted. "We've got you outnumbered. Toss your guns on the ground."

"Who's 'we'?" came a rough voice from the camp.

"Sheriff Jericho Silver and nine deputies with rifles. Do what I said, drop your guns."

Dead silence. "Hurry up, Tucker. You've got five seconds."

He began counting aloud. "Five…four…"

One of the gang members, a scrawny beanpole of a man, tossed away his gun belt.

"Three…two…" Jericho fired a second shot that kicked up dust in front of Beanpole. Another shot from behind the boulder opposite him whined into the ground a foot closer. Yeah, Maddie could shoot a rifle, all right.

Then he spied her black hat bobbing up and down and another shot zinged down into the camp. Beanpole skittered backward and thrust both arms into the air. "Hell, Tuck, they've got us surrounded."

One of the gang fired three quick shots at Maddie's hat but quit when a rifle shot cracked from another direction. The man tossed away his weapon.

"Tucker?" Jericho yelled. "Throw your gun over by the others."

A *thunk* told him the outlaw had obeyed. That's two men disarmed, he thought. Three more to go. He hoped to goodness Maddie stayed out of the line of fire.

Almost in answer, a rifle bullet skimmed into the fire pit, then a few seconds later another popped from a different direction. Good girl! Maddie was circling.

With his foot Jericho waggled the pine branch with his hat perched on it, quietly crept some yards away, and fired two more shots.

Another gun belt plopped down near the others. Two more left. He crept another ten feet to his left and opened fire again. More rifle fire cracked from behind Maddie's black hat.

"Okay, Silver," Tucker yelled. "Call off your men." Another gun belt skidded into the pile, followed by a rifle and two more revolvers. Four figures crept forward, hands in the air, followed by a tall paunchy fellow. Tucker.

"Toss all your firearms over behind the rocks," Jericho ordered.

When the thuds and clanks ceased, the gang milled awkwardly around the fire and Jericho stood up. "Now sit down," he yelled.

Pointing his Winchester at Tucker's chest, he started down the hill. "Pick up their weapons, men," he called to his imaginary deputies. He heard a scrape and then sounds like something being dragged across the ground. Maddie was collecting the guns. *God bless that woman!*

"Sing out when you've got 'em all, men."

He waited, eyeing the ragtag bunch huddled below him. Only Tucker showed no fear. Beanpole and a short, fat kid sat with their heads down on their knees, passing a mashed cigarette back and forth between them.

"Got 'em all, Sheriff," came a raspy voice from the boulder nearest him.

"You backin' me up, Deputy?"

"Yo," the 'deputy' yelled.

Good work, Mrs. Detective.

Jericho walked carefully down into the camp. Behind him something scraped against a rock and he heard a grumbly voice. "I am covering your back, Sheriff."

Then she made the mistake of standing upright to aim her Winchester.

"Get your horses," Jericho snapped at the seated men. "Mount up and stay put or you'll get a bullet in your back. I'm taking you back to stand trial."

The men shuffled off toward their horses. All except Tucker, who stood eyeing Maddie.

"Why, that's nuthin' but a kid," he shouted. From inside his coat he pulled a pistol and sent a shot toward her.

Maddie yelped and went down. Tucker then took aim at Jericho.

Two gunshots split the air. Tucker spun away, holding one arm. Jericho took a bullet hip-high, but he managed to stay upright and aim his rifle. The shot whanged off a boulder instead of nailing Tucker.

Tucker staggered to his horse and with a whoop, all five of the outlaws thundered away from the camp. Jericho loosed a volley of words that would fry a nun's ear. He sent a few shots after them, but the riders were already out of range. Dammit, he'd lost them.

Blood soaked his shirt and his jeans. It felt like a white-hot knife was chewing into his hip and he struggled to breathe through the agony.

"Maddie?" he shouted.

"Y-yes?"

"Are you hurt?"

"Y-yes."

God, she'd been shot. He swung his bloody leg forward, fell, and clawed his way on his hands and knees up to where she lay.

"Where are you hit?" Jericho demanded.

"My leg. Above my knee." Her voice was tight with pain.

He felt up her trouser leg until she sucked in her breath and his fingers felt something warm and sticky.

"Jericho, are y-you wounded, too?"

"Yeah. Got a bullet somewhere in my hip."

She let out a shaky breath. "What are we going to do now?"

He groaned aloud. "Hell, if I knew that, I'd be doing it."

"I'm afraid I cannot walk," she whispered.

"I know that. I'm gonna carry you down to the fire, see how bad hurt we are. Come on, put your arms around my neck."

"But you cannot—"

"Don't tell me what I can't do," he retorted. "Just shut up and hang on." He bent over her, lifted her hands to his neck and lurched to his feet. Gritting his teeth against the molten fire in his hip, he stumbled in jerky steps down to the camp. He laid her down, dug out his pocketknife and slit her trouser leg above her knee.

In the firelight he could see the blood. "Maddie, looks like the bullet went clean through your thigh right above the knee, but it left an ugly path." He snaked the bandanna from around his neck and bound it tight around the ragged hole. Blood soaked through before he finished tying the knot.

Then he stripped off his shirt and dropped his jeans. "Where's my bullet wound?"

"Near your hip bone," she said with maddening calm. "In the fleshy part. I think the bullet is still in there."

Damn. He yanked up his trousers and sat down to sort out what to do. They were probably forty miles from help, but both of them were wounded and losing blood. They had to get themselves back to Smoke River.

"We'll have to ride," he said at last.

"I thought so." She sounded near tears and he didn't blame her one bit. When the chips were down, she'd been fearless, but now...

Now they were in real trouble.

"Listen, Maddie, I'll go get the horses. Maybe there's some of that painkiller left in my saddlebag."

He propped her close to the fire and dragged himself past the boulders and up the hillside to where the horses waited. When he reached them his hands shook and he was sweating, but he knew what he had to do. He lifted his saddlebags off Dancer and sent the mare off with a slap on its rump.

"Go for help, girl. Go back to Smoke River." The horse pounded off into the darkness.

Leading her horse, Jericho stumbled back down to where Maddie lay. His thigh felt like it was on fire, but he clamped his jaw shut and reached out to help her stand. She clenched her teeth and her breath hissed in, but she didn't say a word.

By the time he wrestled her into the saddle, it

felt like a red-hot poker was boring into his hip. He clamped his jaw hard, pulled himself up behind her and wrapped his good arm across her middle.

"Take the reins, Maddie. I sent my horse back to town. Follow Dancer's tracks. Walk her slow and easy so we don't lose too much blood. Understand?"

"Yes." Now her voice sounded unnaturally calm and he bent to one side and gave her a sharp look. Her eyes were wide, her face gray. She was hurt and frightened, and probably sick to death of the West and himself in particular, but she looked into his eyes and tried to smile.

A little knot of warmth settled in his chest. Dammit all, Madison O'Donnell was one helluva woman.

Chapter Eleven

Mile after agonizing mile Maddie rode with Jericho at her back, pointing out the trail she could not begin to see and murmuring encouragement in her ear. "Keep it up, Maddie. You're doing just fine."

"Impossible," she muttered. "Jericho, I hardly know where I'm going."

"Don't worry, the horse does. We'll make it back just fine."

"You are not just saying that to keep up my spirits, are you? I would hate that."

"I wouldn't lie to you, Maddie. We've got a long way to go, but we can do it."

Maddie snuffled. For the last hour she had been weeping silently, and now her nose was running in a most unladylike manner.

"Gettin' kinda dusty. Pull your bandanna up over your nose and mouth."

She yanked up the square of blue printed cotton to cover her mouth, then used the tail to mop at her tears. He knew she was crying; no doubt he could feel her uneven breathing against his chest.

"Is your leg hurting?"

She gave a choked laugh. "I don't know. I'm so tired I can't feel it anymore."

He said nothing, just pointed out a faint hoofprint to the left. She pulled the reins accordingly.

As the miles stretched on, she began to develop a new appreciation for the taciturn sheriff. He was still bleeding. She could feel his upper thigh, warm and sticky, pressed against her hip, and every so often he gave a muffled groan, but he just kept urging the horse forward.

Finally, when she was thinking up ways to tell him she could not go on one more mile, they stopped to water and rest the horse. Her leg throbbed relentlessly and it took all her strength just to move it, but he made her get down and stretch out on the grass. All she wanted to do was curl up on a nice, soft bed and sleep for a week.

Twenty minutes later, Jericho grasped her elbow, maneuvered her back into the saddle and dragged himself up behind her.

They rode on.

How she wished Jericho's clever ruse had worked; at least they would have something to show for their efforts besides bullet wounds and blood-soaked clothing. She had wanted to help, and perhaps she had, despite everything. He almost did capture the gang, and he did it with her help. Of course, when Tucker recognized she was not a real deputy their plan was blown to smithereens. But she had helped, up to a point, had she not? The thought brought a thin-lipped smile and a tiny glow of satisfaction.

She most certainly was not at home in the West, but she wanted the sheriff to think well of her. He might not like her, but she was beginning to feel that the respect of this man was worth gaining. Respect was better than liking.

Jericho grunted at her back. "Maddie? What the devil are you thinkin' about? You're grinning like riding ten hours in the dark is amusing."

"I was remembering when I was twelve years old and tricked a bunch of rowdy boys who were stealing apples from a neighbor's orchard."

"Yeah? How'd you do that?" His voice sounded drowsy but at least she'd stirred his interest.

"I dressed up like a scarecrow and jumped out from behind a tree. Scared them half to death. They ran off, and I gathered up the all apples they dropped."

"Pretty clever."

"Maybe not. I wasn't smart enough to stay quiet about it. Papa laughed and laughed, but my mother confined me to my room for three days."

He said nothing. She could tell from the hitch in his breathing that he was having trouble staying conscious. Probably that's why he kept asking questions.

"Jericho?"

"Yeah?"

"What did you do with all those weapons they tossed down?"

"Stashed them in a safe place."

"Where?"

"Inside a burned-out pine."

How in the world had this man with a bullet lodged in his hip managed to hoist a bunch of heavy rifles and revolvers up into a hollow tree?

"When we get back to town I'll send Sandy back to get them."

Maddie bit her lip. If they ever *did* reach town.

The thick blackness surrounding them began to lighten just enough to make out the shaggy outlines of trees and the meandering river they followed. Maddie closed her eyes for a moment and listened to the burbling water.

She longed for a bath and clean clothes. And a hairbrush. City things, she admitted. The thought of bathing in a creek made her shiver.

"Maddie?"

"Yes?"

"Think we'd better stop. I'm real dizzy. Feel like I'm gonna throw up." He reined in the horse, dismounted and stumbled off a few yards. She could hear him retching, and her stomach clenched. There could not be much food in his belly, but he kept vomiting for what seemed like hours. The sound brought tears to her eyes.

"Jericho, do you need help?"

"No. Stay put, Maddie. I'll be all right in a min—"

He broke off abruptly.

She felt awful, but at least she was not sick to her stomach. Her entire body ached, her wounded leg especially. Her eyes felt grainy and hot, and her thighs were cramping.

"Sheriff, perhaps we should rest here awhile."

No answer.

"Jericho?"

He walked toward her, wiping his sleeve across his mouth. "Got to keep goin'. Got to warn the bank in town not to ship that gold tomorrow."

The gold shipment. Heavens, she'd almost forgotten the thousands of dollars in gold dust the Smoke River Bank had entrusted to Wells Fargo.

Jericho pulled himself into the saddle behind her. "Let's move on."

Her throat tightened at the tiredness in his voice.

They rode on for another two hours while Maddie fought down a growing fear. What if Jericho's wound became infected? Could he die from loss of blood? She kicked the mare into a canter.

Without warning, he sagged sideways and Maddie reined up beside the river they were following. "We will stop here to rest, Jericho. Do not argue."

He didn't. He jockeyed himself out of the saddle, his face white and strained, and laid out a blanket close to the riverbank. He stumbled over to Maddie, dragged her out of the saddle and laid her down on top of the rough wool, then collapsed beside her. Within minutes he was asleep, his arm wrapped protectively around her waist.

Jericho had no idea how long he slept, but when he opened his eyes it was full dark and he knew he was burning up with fever. Must be his wound was festering.

Maddie lay curled up beside him, still sleeping. Very gingerly he rolled away from her and sat up. Something at the edge of the blanket caught his eye. What the—

A scant foot from Maddie's head sat a tight-woven willow basket holding a whiskey bottle filled with some kind of liquid. Beside it lay a bundle of tree moss and a stack of soft deerskin strips.

"Maddie, wake up." He touched her shoulder. "Our Indian friend's been here."

"What did he take this time?" she mumbled.

"Nothing. He left something for us."

He worked the cork out of the bottle and sniffed at the contents. "Willow-bark tea. The Indians use it for fever." He tipped it into his mouth and gulped down four big swallows. It tasted bitter, but he had to smile. He couldn't begin to guess how the old Indian knew of their difficulty, but he was sure grateful. He didn't even want to wonder why he hadn't heard any footsteps.

"Lie still, Maddie. I'm going to bandage your leg." He unwrapped the bloodstained bandanna around the wound, packed the torn flesh with half the moss and bound it tight using the strips of deerskin.

When he finished, he lay facedown beside her, tugged his shirt free of his jeans, and slid them down a few inches. "Put the rest of that moss on my hip, would you? Then snug it up with those deerskin strips."

Without a word, she bent over him and rucked up his shirt. He liked the feel of her hands on his flesh, but he was too tired to think much beyond getting them back to town.

Before they remounted, Jericho left a pound of good jerky and two cans of peaches on the river bank as a gift.

It was growing light enough to see now. They headed away from the river, and just when Maddie knew she could not ride one more mile, Jericho suddenly leaned forward.

"Pull up," he rasped.

She hesitated. "Why?"

"Look ahead. Riders comin'."

Her heart plummeted into her belly and she hauled back on the reins.

"Four riders," he breathed. "Comin' fast."

She tried to keep her voice steady. "We should find cover." She reined off the trail, heading toward a stand of cottonwoods near a bend in the river.

"Wait!" he ordered sharply.

"But—"

"That's Sandy. I recognize one of his horses. And Doc Graham is with him." He tightened his arm around her waist.

Dust plumed behind the mounted men. Jericho waited until they were closer, then dismounted and walked unsteadily forward to meet them.

The two other riders turned out to be Colonel Wash Halliday and Rooney Cloudman, the half-Indian scout who used to ride with the colonel. All four men reined in their mounts, and Doc Graham and Sandy immediately scrambled off their horses.

"I knew somethin' was wrong the minute Dancer came into town last night," Sandy said. "Figured you got into some kinda trouble so I deputized Mr. Cloudman and Colonel Halliday."

"Good work," Jericho said, his voice grainy with exhaustion. "I stashed some weapons a ways back. One of you could go get them. They're hidden in a rotted-out pine about five miles from where the railroad runs close to a circle of big river boulders."

The colonel and Cloudman reined away and Jericho turned to the doctor. "Mrs. O'Donnell's shot in the leg, Doc, and I took a bullet in my hip."

Dr. Graham, a tall, somewhat stooped man with streaks of silver in his gray hair, dismounted and poked Jericho in the chest with one bony forefinger. "Lie down, son. Let me dig out that bullet."

He pointed to the saddle blanket Sandy was spreading on the ground. "Not going to be much fun, Johnny, but I guess you know that. If it makes any difference, I brought some good whiskey."

Jericho downed two big gulps and watched Maddie limp toward them. "Give her some too, will ya, Doc?"

"Later," Graham said. "You're the one with the fever."

Jericho pinned him with a look. "Not later, Doc. Now." He pushed the older man's hand gripping the quart bottle toward Maddie. "I said to give her some."

Doc's gray eyes suddenly went wide. "*Her?* What do you mean, 'her'?"

"He means me," Maddie said at his elbow. "Madison O'Donnell."

Doc Graham's gray eyebrows shot up. "Well, I'll be…you a drinking lady, ma'am?"

"A little," she said with a shaky laugh. "Maybe more, now that I've been shot. I would drink anything to dull this pain." She lifted the whiskey bottle out of his hand, upended it against her lips, and gulped down two big swallows.

"Save some for Johnny," the physician cautioned. He arranged the contents of his black bag on the clean towel he spread out on the blanket. "Now, boy, roll over and let's take a look." He bent down to inspect Jericho's bloody back.

"I'm right sorry to keep you waiting, Miz O'Donnell, but this lad's gotta be first." Doc knelt on Jericho's other side, a shiny steel probe on his hand.

Maddie settled herself by his side and offered him the whiskey bottle. Doc splashed it over the wound, then bent low and went to work.

"God," Jericho gasped through clenched teeth. "Feels like you're diggin' around with a…" He sputtered out another curse. "Pitchfork."

Maddie bit her lip.

Sandy paced around them in a circle. "Hey," the deputy suddenly burst out. "Aren't those my boots?"

"Shut up, Sandy," Jericho groaned. With Doc's next probe his body convulsed. Maddy grasped his hand and held it so tight her knuckles hurt.

"Thanks," he breathed. The next probe had him writhing again.

"Ouch! Damn, Maddie," he gasped. "I'm gonna hurt your hand."

Maddie closed her eyes but maintained her hold. "Jericho, this is hard to watch."

"Then don't," he snapped.

"Do not order me around, Sheriff. I will do as I please."

He gave a low moan. "Yeah, I know."

She tightened her grip, then leaned down and spoke near his ear. "Damn right."

He started to laugh, then sucked in a breath.

"Found it!" Doc chortled. "Now to get it out of there."

He splashed more whiskey over Jericho's back. He hissed and squirmed, but Maddie held on.

The physician poked around with an oversize pair of steel tweezers. "Ha! Got it!" He waved the tweezers in the air. "Always like this part the best."

Jericho closed his eyes and took a full breath for the first time in the last twenty minutes. He noticed Maddie still had her fingers laced with his. All at once he wanted to bring her small, capable hand to his lips. Must be the whiskey making his brain go soft.

He felt an even stronger urge to roll over and pull her into his arms. "Real good whiskey," he murmured.

"Now, Miz O'Donnell, let's see that leg of yours."

Maddie stretched out her blood-encrusted jeans, and Doc spread the seam Jericho had ripped to expose her knee and lifted away the moss.

"Ah. Nice clean wound." He sloshed whiskey over the bullet hole. "Now it's sterile, too."

It felt like a bath of fire and tears stung into her eyes. "Thank you," she whispered.

"Who wrapped this up for you?"

"Jericho did."

Doc Graham nodded. "Nice work, Johnny. Maybe you shoulda been a doctor instead of the sheriff."

Sandy and Doc both laughed. Maddie noted that Jericho did not.

With a final comforting pat on her shoulder, Doc rolled up his instruments in the towel and stuffed it back into his black leather bag. "Now, children," he ordered. "Let's get you to my little hospital in Smoke River."

Chapter Twelve

Jericho's back hurt as if the tines of a hay fork were biting into his flesh. Sandy rode on one side of them with Doc on the other, and before another hour passed, Rooney Cloudman and Colonel Halliday galloped up with the discarded weapons rolled up in two horse blankets and tied behind their saddles.

The colonel took a long look at Jericho's arm wrapped tight around Maddie's waist, then flicked Cloudman a look. Rooney looked steadily at the trail ahead and didn't crack a smile. Jericho wanted to punch them both.

Maddie didn't say much for the entire ride back to Smoke River.

Main Street was deserted when they reached town, probably because of the afternoon heat. Sandy stopped at the jail and took charge of the stash of guns. Rooney and the colonel headed for home, and Doc, Jericho and Maddie rode slowly to Sarah Rose's boardinghouse behind the honeysuckle-swathed white picket fence. Doc's hospital, as the graying physician called it. He boarded there, and the two large upstairs rooms served as his infirmary.

Mrs. Rose met them at the gate, her lips pinched. "What on earth?"

"Guess we're gonna open up the infirmary again, Sarah," Doc said. "Johnny's gotten himself shot and this young lady needs some attention, as well."

The gray-bunned widow shot Maddie a look, then shooed Jericho upstairs with the doctor. "Bet you'd like a bath, wouldn't you, um…Miss."

Maddie could have kissed her.

"I'll heat up some water, dearie. You come on back to my kitchen and strip off those dirty clothes." She shook her head and tsked. "I can't believe Johnny made you wear boots and jeans, but I've given up trying to figure out that man."

Maddie was too tired to explain. Instead, she toed off Sandy's overlarge boots, stripped off the filthy, blood-soaked jeans and her sweaty shirt, and sank into the copper hip bath Mrs. Rose filled.

"You related to Johnny in some way?" the elderly woman inquired, peering at Maddie over the top of her glasses.

"No," Maddie said. "I posed as the sheriff's cousin, but you know that he doesn't have a cousin. I am a… I was sent from Chicago to help him."

"I figured something like that." Mrs. Rose chuckled. "I'll bet Johnny wasn't thrilled to find you were a female, was he?"

Maddie had to laugh. "As a matter of fact, he's been furious ever since I stepped off the train."

"Do him good," Mrs. Rose said. "About time he— Oh! My cake's burning!" She wrapped her apron around her hand and snatched a square pan from the oven. "Pshaw, now I'll have to…"

Maddie closed her eyes and blotted out the woman's voice. What she thought about was Jericho Silver. In spite of his brusque responses and the fact that he did not want a woman, even a trained professional Pinkerton detective, interfering in his plans, or his life, she had to admit she liked him.

She liked him very much, in fact. He was short-spoken to the point of rudeness, single-minded to the point of being pigheaded, and stubborn—oh, yes, he was stubborn. Yet she knew she could trust Jericho Silver with her life.

She had never felt that way about a man before, not even her father. Jericho's blue-black eyes could be as hard as coal nuggets, but they always looked straight into hers. Sometimes they looked troubled, or puzzled, or angry, and sometimes, when he thought she wasn't looking, the expression in them was oddly hesitant, as if what she said or did actually mattered to him. Mrs. Rose was right. Jericho was hard to figure out.

But in spite of everything, she did like him. When he looked at her a certain way, or inadvertently brushed his hand against her, a sweet, hot jolt of something settled behind her breastbone.

Doc Graham wanted to check her wounded leg

once more, and Mrs. Rose insisted she stay for supper. "No point in limping into the hotel, now, is there, when you can stay right here?"

Maddie rinsed the soap off her arms and back, feeling clean and decidedly more female for the first time in two days, and dried herself with a thick, oven-warmed towel. Then she donned the yellow seersucker skirt and lace-trimmed shirtwaist Sandy had retrieved from her hotel room and slipped out the back door to visit the mercantile. And the bank.

Later, when she entered the blue-wallpapered dining room on the supporting arm of Doc Graham, she still limped but the bullet wound no longer ached.

The two men at the long mahogany dining table bolted to their feet. One was the graying but still handsome Rooney Cloudman, the retired army scout Jericho had told her about. Rooney seated her with a flourish next to himself. The other man was young, shiny-faced and tongue-tied in her presence.

"Reuben Parry," Doc Graham said by way of introduction. Reuben goggled at Maddie in silence and when she smiled at him, he turned scarlet.

"Where's Johnny?" Rooney demanded.

"Asleep upstairs," Doc explained. "At least I hope he's asleep. Gave him a good dose of laudanum so he'd stop giving me orders."

Two elderly women were also seated at the table, both eyeing Maddie with curiosity. Doc Graham introduced them as retired schoolteachers from Portland, Iris DuPont and her sister, Mrs. Elvira Hinksley.

"What a lovely yellow dress," one remarked. "Don't you agree, Iris?"

"Agree? Of course I agree. Like spring daisies or daffodils. Are you visiting someone in Smoke River, my dear?"

The question caught Maddie off guard. She certainly could not admit she was a Pinkerton agent to them; agents on assignment were instructed to remain strictly incognito. She had evaded the issue with Sarah Rose, even though she knew she could trust the older woman.

"Yes, I am visiting," she lied. "I am visiting my… cousin, Sheriff Silver."

Both women raised silvery eyebrows. "We were not aware Johnny had a cousin," Elvira said.

Johnny again. Half the town seemed to have adopted the sheriff. Maddie unfolded her linen napkin. "Actually, the sheriff is my second cousin. Twice removed." She did hate being dishonest, but at that moment Mrs. Rose caught her gaze and held it just long enough to assure Maddie that her real reason for being in Smoke River was safe.

Mrs. Rose's towheaded young grandson, Mark, marched in with a platter of fried chicken, followed by the landlady herself with a china tureen large enough to float toy boats in. When everyone had filled their plates with chicken and mashed potatoes, Rooney Cloudman lifted his cup for some of the coffee Mrs. Rose was pouring.

"How's Johnny doin', Doc? Looked mighty peaked when you brought him in."

"I'd say he'll probably pull through. He's still un-conscious, though."

"Unconscious?" Maddie blurted. "Why—"

Doc Graham lifted the chicken platter. "Well, Mrs. O'Donnell, in addition to the wound in his back, he's suffering from shock and fever from a nasty infection."

"He will be all right, though, will he not?" To mask her concern and quiet her erratic heartbeat, Maddie sipped from the coffee cup Mrs. Rose had filled.

"Most likely. But one never knows with bullet wounds."

Maddie picked at her supper of chicken and mashed potatoes until she could not stand one more minute of talk about wheat crops or summer toma-toes or the weather. At dinner in Chicago, one might discuss city politics, the Illinois state fair, or Mrs. Ulysses Grant's inauguration ball gown. She had to remind herself Smoke River was a farming commu-nity, full of…well, farmers. She would die of bore-dom in a small country town like this.

As soon as she could, she excused herself and quietly climbed the stairs, pausing on the landing to determine which room was Jericho's. It must be that one, with a faint light showing under the door-way. She slipped inside and then wished she had not.

The lantern was turned down low, casting a soft glow across the still figure on the bed. Jericho lay on his stomach, breathing heavily. A wide swath of white gauze and tape encased him from hip to shoulder blade. No blood showed, but the bandage was sticky with a yellow liquid draining from somewhere underneath.

"Jericho?" she whispered. After what Doc Graham had said, she was growing uneasy. How would she finish her assignment if Jericho…well, until he was well enough to ride?

"Jericho?" she said again. "Sheriff Silver?"

No response. He drew a breath in and expelled it with a harsh sound, but his eyes remained closed. Maddie bent over him.

He smelled of leather and wood smoke and sweat. Movement beneath his lids told her he was dreaming. A china basin of water sat on a nearby table, smelling faintly of peppermint, and a damp cloth was draped on the rim. Someone must have been sponging him off.

Careful not to jar him, she perched on the edge of the bed, dunked the cloth in the basin and wrung it out.

"Jericho, perhaps you can hear me, perhaps not. But I have some things to tell you." She smoothed the cloth over the side of his flushed forehead and across the back of his neck.

"I visited the bank this afternoon. They will delay the gold shipment until we send word."

No response. She rinsed out the cloth and drew it across his bare back above and below the bandage. His skin was so hot! Good gracious, his whole body was on fire. Again she dipped and bathed his face and neck, then his bare arms and shoulders.

"Jericho, I hope you are listening. I know you think I talk too much, but this is important." She waited five heartbeats, hoping for a response—a twitch of a finger, a shrug of his muscular shoulders, anything.

"I have also visited the mercantile. You remember that tall, gawky boy you thought might be Carl Ness's cousin? He is not really Ness's cousin. Or his nephew or anything else. He is just a temporary helper. And…"

She paused to cool the cloth in the basin. "I think that boy might be part of the Tucker gang. For one thing, when I stopped in, he was wearing that red-orange bandanna around his neck, the one we recognized on the train. And for another, I noticed the back of his knuckles on one hand were badly scraped. I believe one our bullets grazed him."

She dipped, squeezed out the water and again smoothed the cloth over his back. "What beautiful skin you have," she murmured. "Though I do not suppose a man cares about such a thing."

She studied the top half of his frame. "In fact, the whole of you is quite pleasing. Your shoulders, especially."

She straightened suddenly. What on earth was she saying?

"Believe me, Jericho," she said on a sigh, "it is no fun talking to you this way. It is much better when you order me around, even when you tease and make jokes. I like it when you do that—it makes our conversations interesting."

More passes with the cooling cloth. "Jericho, I do wish you could hear me. We need to discuss what to do about that boy at the mercantile. Could you arrest him just on suspicion? No, I suppose you would not do that. Another sheriff might, but not you."

She brushed the straggling dark hair off the back of his neck. "But it still bothers me that someone is tipping off the gang about the gold shipments. That, in my opinion, is why we found those outlaws camped so near the railroad tracks."

Jericho's breathing hitched and a moan drifted out of his open mouth.

"Jericho?"

A groan this time.

"Jericho, are you awake? Can you hear me?"

"Hmm," he rumbled.

Maddie's hand shook as she wrung out the cloth. "Jericho? Oh, I do wish you would say something."

"Damn," he rasped.

Her heart skipped at least three beats. "Yes? Yes? Damn what?"

He tried to roll over but gave it up. She leaned down and put her ear close to his mouth. "Damn what?"

"Damn, you smell good."

Maddie jerked upright. Speechless, she stared down at what she had thought was an unconscious man. His dark hair was damp with sweat. Perhaps he was delirious?

"Sheriff," she said in her best no-nonsense voice.

"I am certain that you are awake. Open your eyes and look at me."

He moved not one muscle except for his lips. "Dammit, Maddie, stop nagging."

She almost wept with relief. He was much more alive than he looked lying there on Mrs. Rose's carved walnut bed swathed in bandages. His chiseled features were flushed with fever and his back, under Doc Graham's handiwork, still looked swollen, but he was breathing in and out and even talking.

She knotted her fingers together until they ached. Men could die from gunshot wounds. Had he been delirious with fever when he said she smelled good? Perhaps to a man in his condition, a stack of newspapers would smell good.

Jericho painfully heaved himself over onto his back. "Put a towel under me," he croaked. "Don't want to stain the sheet."

Maddie grabbed a towel from the top of the bureau and folded it in half. With some effort Jericho sat up part way so she could slip it under his back. Then he sank back, exhausted.

"Gettin' shot sure takes the vinegar out of a man."

"Oh!" she exclaimed. "You are not the least bit delirious!"

"Not now, anyway. Had some pretty wild dreams, though. Glad I didn't talk much."

In fact, Jericho hoped to hell he hadn't said a single word. He'd dreamed about Maddie. In his fevered state, his feelings about her were no longer puzzling, they were as plain as freckles on a kid's nose. Downright explicit, even.

He forced his eyes open and looked up at her. Her mouth was doing funny things, looking kinda trembly, and then she caught her lower lip between her teeth.

Jericho winced. "You upset about something?"

Maddie scrambled off the bed and paced back and forth between the bed and the window. He noted the limp in her gait.

"Why, no, I am not upset," she said, her voice tight. "My associate is almost killed and I—" She broke off. "Of course I am upset."

Her cheeks were turning the prettiest shade of pink. Hell, maybe he was delirious; he wanted to run his tongue over her flushed skin.

She tramped unevenly to his bedside, planted her hands on her hips and glared down at him with a look that could kindle a campfire. He started to laugh but a white-hot rod of pain jabbed into his back and he caught his breath. It took a full minute before he could speak.

"Maddie, sit down."

She dropped onto the bed beside him and the rod drove into him again.

"Now, then, Mrs. Detective. Why are you upset?"

She leaned down. Her usually clear eyes looked wet. Tears? Tears from his starched and proper lady detective?

"Because," she began. "Because…oh, I don't know."

Something fluttered beneath his breastbone. He reached up, grasped her shoulders and tugged her down until they were nose to nose. Her warm breath fanned his mouth.

What was he doing?

He wanted to touch her. Taste her.

He lifted his head slightly and grazed her lips with his. She went absolutely still, but once he'd started, he didn't want to stop. An overpowering hunger washed over him and he pulled her forward, deepened the kiss, then deepened it again. A rush of dizzying sensation made him acutely aware of every tight, sizzling nerve in his body.

When he released her, she straightened and held his gaze with a question in her eyes. "Why did you do that?"

"To be honest, I don't really know." He cleared his throat. "But I'm glad I did." More than glad, he was burning up with wanting her.

Someone rapped sharply on the closed door. "Miz O'Donnell?" a young voice called. "Deputy's here to walk you home, ma'am. You 'bout ready?"

Maddie rose and cracked open the door. "Thank you, Mark. Tell him I will come down directly."

"How's the sheriff doin'? Ever'body in town wants to know."

Maddie pondered the boy's words. The people here really cared about Sheriff Silver. Was it because in a town this small everyone knew everyone and all about their troubles, as well? She sensed it was more than that. Jericho Silver was valued, even revered, because of the man he was.

"The sheriff is…" She glanced over her shoulder at the motionless form on the bed. His eyes were closed, his breathing irregular. He looked like he was asleep, but she could tell something troubled him; his lips were thinned with pain.

"The sheriff is growing stronger by the hour, Mark. He is sleeping now. You will tell the others, won't you?"

"Sure will, ma'am. Thanks."

Maddie watched the boy clatter down the stairs and then heard the murmur of voices below. A woman laughed. "That's our Johnny." Mrs. Rose's voice.

Maddie stepped to the bedside. One of Jericho's arms stretched along his side, palm up. Gently she touched his fingers. His hand closed around hers, then relaxed in sleep.

Suddenly she felt like crying.

On the short walk from the boardinghouse to the hotel, Sandy proved more talkative than she thought she could stand. The warm night air smelled of honeysuckle, and the quiet shutting-up-shop sounds along the main street sent a sudden melancholy through her. As a girl she had always hated it when activity stopped, when children were called in to supper from games of jump rope and Red Rover, when the stores and the candy shop and the bakery shut their doors and the proprietors went home to their families.

Now, everything was quiet, as if the town had gone to sleep and everything was at peace. Well, not everything.

Jericho's strained mouth had told her that the sheriff was not at peace. She caught her breath. Was it because he had kissed her and had not liked it? Or perhaps, she wondered with an odd ache in her chest, perhaps he *had* liked it but he did not *want* to like it?

After a long minute, she became aware of Sandy's continuing one-sided conversation. "Can't say how long the sheriff's been in Smoke River, ma'am. He's been sheriff ever since I was a kid in knee pants. All I ever wanted to do when I grew up was be exactly like him."

The deputy coughed and studied the toes of his boots. "Guess that's why I'm glad he's not tracking the Tucker boys on his own."

"Do you want to help him?"

"I sure do, but he won't let me. When he's out huntin' down a fellow, he won't hardly let me out of the jail, so to speak."

Maddie mm-hmmed and asked, "Why not?"

"Sheriff's funny that way," the deputy said slowly. "He needs a deputy, but he gets real upset if I get hurt."

Maddie nodded. She understood. It was because of that Indian girl at the orphanage.

"When I was growin' up, talk was that when Jericho was about twelve years old, Tom Roper found him hidin' in the livery stable one night when it was rainin' hard. He was scared and hungry, and Tom fed him and gave him a job muckin' out the stable."

"A job?" Of course, she reflected. Something to hold on to. Something useful to do with one's life.

"Tom said he was as scrawny as a scarecrow, but he worked hard and was real smart. Didn't have any family. Learned himself readin' and writin' and started helpin' out around town. You know, keepin' things peaceful. Taught himself to shoot pretty good and he was always real fair-minded, but he sure was tough. Even when he was outnumbered, he never backed down. He just kinda adopted the town, you might say."

"Go on," Maddie breathed. "Tell me more."

"Got elected sheriff when he was about my age, around twenty. Guess he's about thirty, now."

She stuffed down a laugh. Jericho Silver was thirty going on seventy-five. A cool, calculating loner, with a heart packed in ice.

But he had kissed her.

And now? What about Mr. Loner, now?

They reached the hotel lobby, and Sandy conducted her up the staircase to her door. All at once the young man looked stricken.

"You won't tell the sheriff I told you all these things, will ya?"

"Most certainly not. You have my word. And you will not tell him I asked all these questions, will you?"

"Oh, no, ma'am. Lotsa women ask me about

Sheriff Silver, but you're the only one I ever told anything to."

Maddie turned the key in the lock. "Why me, Sandy?"

The young deputy blinked. "Uh, well, I guess it's, um…because I think he likes you."

Maddie narrowed her eyes. "Why on earth would you think that? Sheriff Silver has been condescending and short-tempered and bossy since the first minute of our acquaintance."

Sandy opened his mouth, then shut it. Tipping his wide-brimmed felt hat he sidled past her and headed down the stairs.

"Dunno, Miz O'Donnell," he called over his shoulder. "Just horse sense, I guess."

Horse sense! What did that mean?

Why had she had let Sandy ramble on and on about the sheriff? She longed to put the man out of her mind completely, finish this assignment and go back to Chicago where she belonged.

Didn't she?

She pushed open her hotel room door and marched inside.

He likes me, indeed. The last thing in the world she wanted was an attachment to a man. Attachments led to marrying and that led to the kind of prison she had sworn to avoid for the rest of her life.

Tomorrow, she resolved, she and the sheriff were going to reestablish their original relationship. Being Jericho's adversary was much safer than being his… what? His friend?

But he had kissed her!

She spun away from the door, sat down hard on the bed, and dropped her head into her hands.

Jericho is more than a friend, Maddie-girl. And you know it.

Chapter Thirteen

Maddie stepped up onto the veranda of Sarah Rose's boardinghouse to find Doc Graham rocking in the porch swing.

"Come to see Johnny, have you? Well, you can save yourself a climb up those stairs, Miz O'Donnell. Johnny's not here."

"Not here? What do you mean, he's not here?"

"What I mean is the minute he could manage to get himself dressed and navigate down the stairs, there was no holding him," Doc Graham grumbled.

"But he had a fever!"

"Yep. Probably still does. He's maybe over at the jail, makin' Sandy's life miserable."

But at the jail, the deputy shook his head. "Sorry, ma'am," he said with a shrug. "Sheriff's out back. Practicing, I reckon."

"Practicing! Practicing what?"

Sandy ushered her out the back door of the jail

and pointed across a stubbly brown field. "Look over yonder, ma'am."

Maddie fixed her gaze on the tall, lean figure across the expanse of dry bunchgrass. He had his back to her, facing what looked like a broomstick planted in the ground with a shiny tin can nailed to the tip, at which he was leveling a revolver. Three shots cracked into the still morning air and thudded into the hillock behind the can.

"Dammit!" Jericho rubbed the back of his neck with his left hand. She noted he was using his right hand to hold the revolver, but the weapon was wavering unsteadily.

Maddie planted her high-buttoned leather shoes on the field, marched through the tufts of scarlet fireweed, and crunched to where the sheriff stood.

"Jericho?"

He made a half turn toward her and lowered the weapon to his side. "What are you doing out here, Maddie?"

"I came to find you. What are *you* doing out here? What about your bullet wound?"

"Hurts," he snapped.

"And what about your injured hand?"

"Hurts," he repeated.

"Then why—"

"Because I'm the sheriff here. You ever hear of a sheriff worth his salt who can only shoot with one hand?"

"But when we—" She stopped abruptly. "You

fired your rifle when we surrounded the Tucker gang. That must have hurt, too."

"Not too much. With a rifle you can use two hands. A revolver's different. I've been working my hand to strengthen it, but I need to do some target practice." He turned back to the broomstick.

"Jericho, we need to talk."

"Yeah, we do." He would not look at her.

"When?"

"Give me another hour out here, then I'll meet you at the boardinghouse."

By the time Jericho quit banging away at the tin can, his hip wound throbbed, his arm ached like a horse had kicked it and a buzzing was starting in his head. It evaporated when he saw Maddie sitting in the swing on Mrs. Rose's porch, her legs curled up under her yellow skirt. His breath hitched.

Lacy petticoats peeked out from under the flounces. Jericho swallowed hard, tramped up the steps, and stood looking at her while she rocked back and forth in the swing.

"Why are you staring at me like that, Sheriff?"

He dropped his gaze to the painted plank floor. "Didn't realize I was, I guess." He winced at the lie. From the instant he opened Mrs. Rose's front gate, he'd done nothing but drink in the vision she made in that ruffly yellow dress. Damn, she looked good enough to eat.

Or kiss.

He couldn't remember clearly how it had happened, but last night when his mouth met hers something inside him stretched tight and began to fray.

"Jericho, I think we need to talk."

Oh, hell, here it came. She was going to make a fuss about that kiss. Carefully he leaned his shoulder against the porch post and braced himself.

"Yeah? What about?"

"About the Tucker gang. About our plan."

So she wasn't going to crawl all over him about kissing her. He expelled a breath of relief and then frowned. Then he grew puzzled. And after that he got downright annoyed.

Didn't she remember he had kissed her? Didn't it matter to her? It sure as hell mattered to him.

"What plan?"

She stopped the motion of the swing. "I thought about it last night," she announced.

Jericho froze against the post. "Thought about what?"

The swing lurched into action again. "About what we should do next."

He fought a stab of apprehension, but she rattled on. "I have an idea. A brilliant idea."

For a full minute he studied the woman moving back and forth in front of him. And then something in his brain fell into place.

"I've got a plan, too."

She looked up at him with widening green eyes. "Oh? Tell me."

"I'm going after the gang again. I know how to get close enough to get the drop on them.

The swing stopped with a clunk. "But the Tucker gang knows you on sight!"

"And they know you, too, Maddie. They've seen you on the train looking like a lady, and they've seen you in their camp, looking like a boy."

"Only a fool would try to capture five rough, un-principled men alone."

"Yeah, well I've done it before. That's how I work, alone. How I've always worked."

"But why? You're respected in this town. You could have help."

"I know there's men in town who'd ride with me, form a posse. But...well, they've got wives and kids. I'd never want a kid to grow up without a father, like I did."

Her lips thinned, then opened. "I came out here to help you, Jericho Silver, and that is exactly what I am going to do."

"Yeah," he conceded. "But remember you told me your jobs before were to gather information, not back somebody up."

Maddie stared at him. "I have proved I can ride a horse, and you know I can shoot. I am coming with you."

"No, you're not. First off, I hate to say this, but you don't ride well enough to keep up. Second, it's dangerous."

"More dangerous than pretending you're ten armed men instead of only one?"

He just looked at her.

She kicked the swing into motion again. "Jericho, I am not afraid of danger. You know that."

"Yeah, I do know that. I'm sorry to say you've got more intelligence and more grit and more plain damn foolish courage than any woman I've ever known."

"So, why won't you let me—"

"Because I'm the sheriff here, and a sheriff can't afford to be plain damn foolish, that's why."

"It is not foolish. It is simply a matter of practicality. I can shoot. You cannot. At least not with your right hand."

He shoved off the porch post and stepped in close. "Maddie, shut up and listen to me. You've scoured out some vital information about those gold shipments, maybe even identified one of the gang, that young kid at the mercantile with the red bandanna. And—"

"And I backed you up," she interjected. "Twice."

Jericho sucked in a gulp of air. "Yeah, you did. I owe you some thanks. But there's a limit—"

"A limit?" Her voice rose. "What limit? I have been valuable to you."

He nodded, thinking hard about what he wanted to say and how to say it. "You're still valuable to me. That's why I don't want you along."

Her face paled. "Just exactly what does that mean, Sheriff? I am fired? Is that it?"

"In a way, yeah."

"Why?" she demanded. "You owe me the truth, Jericho Silver."

Oh, hell, here it came. The truth was that he didn't

want Maddie in danger. He hadn't wanted it all along, but after last night, wanting to keep on kissing her after he'd tasted her mouth, it was even more important.

"I don't want you to get hurt."

She gazed at him with the oddest expression, half outrage, half disbelief. "Why?" she asked again. "Why do you think of this now, after all we have been through together?"

Hell's popcorn balls, he wasn't exactly sure. But she deserved as much honesty as he could muster. "Because we've come damn close to getting killed. Getting killed may be part of a sheriff's job, but it's not part of a lady detective's."

She opened her mouth, probably to scream at him, and he raised his hand to shut her up.

"Don't argue, Maddie. It gives me a headache."

"Very well, I will not argue." She clipped her words so short they rattled out of her mouth like buckshot. "Instead, I will make you a proposition."

She didn't notice the sudden twitch in his spine at the word.

"If you are unsuccessful, if you return from your foolish, brave, stupid venture with no prisoners, and if you are not wounded, as you are now, then you must promise to follow *my* plan. Or at least listen to it. Is it a deal?"

She waited for his answer with sparks flashing in her eyes. Well, why not? He'd done this before. He knew his ruse could be successful, given a bit of luck. He'd bring in the Tucker boys sure as daisies bloomed in the spring.

He let out a long sigh. "Okay, it's a deal."

Maddie stood up slowly and moved three steps to where he stood propped against the white-painted porch post.

"Sheriff..." She extended her hand. "If you shake hands on it, I know you will not break your word."

Jericho hesitated. Oh, what the hell. Chances were he'd bring in the Tucker gang and never have to hear about Maddie's new plan.

He took her small, warm hand in his. The touch of her soft skin against his palm prodded his heartbeat into double time. He was glad, very glad, that Maddie would be staying in Smoke River, where she'd be safe.

At the same time, his heart began to pound violently. He had to admit he hadn't got the sand to ask himself the question he knew he should ask: *Why* was he glad?

He just knew he was. Right now he figured that's all that mattered.

"Help yourself to Sandy's jailhouse coffee while I'm gone. That boy's dyin' to keep his eye on you."

Chapter Fourteen

The next four days were the longest Maddie could ever remember. The sun rose every morning, a fat golden ball that heated her hotel room, the town, the jailhouse where Sandy made coffee for her every day, even Mrs. Rose's front porch where she sat making notes in her log about bank shipments and the Wells Fargo agent that brought them to town.

By afternoon, she usually began to wilt. Her camisole plastered itself to her skin, her whalebone stays poked into her flesh, her starched petticoats went limp and got tangled between her ankles.

And her eyes, merciful heaven! Her eyes itched and burned after hours spent watching the road into town for a glimpse of the tall, lean sheriff of Smoke River.

She visited the dressmaker's neat shop next to the bakery and bought a new wide-brimmed straw hat, trimmed with a yellow ribbon, and another shirt-waist with lace down the front, in pale blue dimity. She found, however, that new clothes did not help.

Nothing helped. She could not believe she missed that maddening, set-in-his-ways, unmovable man so much. But she did.

Maddie, what is happening to you?

Every morning Rita heaped her breakfast plate with scrambled eggs and crispy fried potatoes and laced her coffee with Jericho's favorite brandy, and each evening the waitress saved her a piece of the sheriff's favorite chocolate cake.

No matter what she did, she could not stop thinking about the determined, foolishly courageous sheriff of Smoke River.

Rita talked about him constantly, how she'd tried her best to fatten him up when he was "just a scrawny, lost kid," and what Jericho had given her last Christmas, a real cashmere shawl. The man was a puzzle, remote and hard-edged to the point of rudeness, yet gentle toward those he cared about.

Sandy talked and talked and talked while she sipped coffee in the sheriff's office every morning. Maddie learned where the swimming hole was, and how Ellie Johnson, the schoolteacher, had married her handsome Federal Marshal after twenty-nine years of spinsterhood. How practically everyone in town admired their sheriff's bravery and skill and unflappable calm under fire. She learned more about Jericho in four days than she had ever known about her employer, Allan Pinkerton.

Before each day drew to a dusky close, she was a bundle of anxieties, and nights in her stifling hotel room were sleepless ordeals. She lay awake for hours imagining Jericho lying wounded and alone.

Each bright sunshine-washed morning she lay listening to the sounds of life in this small town, the clank and jingle of wagons rattling down the main street, the rhythmic swish-swish of the barber methodically sweeping off the board sidewalk in front of his shop, the excited clamor of children allowed to buy a cookie or a tart from the bakery.

Life in Smoke River seemed a thousand miles away from the bustling city she was used to. The days meandered by at a snail's pace, leaving her far too much time to think.

Tonight, lying in bed, she mulled over that kiss Jericho had given her. It was odd that he did not seem to remember it; his behavior the next day had not changed one bit. However, she did note a new tension between them that had not been there before. Perhaps he had been delirious that night and he really did not remember kissing her.

But *she* remembered it. She remembered every single second of it. The touch of his lips on hers had startled her, but then his gentle but insistent pressure had nudged her entire being into flame, like a smoldering campfire when a drop of kerosene falls onto the coals.

She remembered how he tasted, like coffee and something hot and sweet. Peppermint. How her insides had begun to tremble and how afterward her lips had felt swollen and hot.

Unconsciously she touched her forefinger to her

mouth. Even when she was married, her husband's kiss had never felt like that. It was shocking. And disturbing and thrilling and unnerving and wonderful all at the same time.

You silly goose, it was just one kiss.

And she wanted another one.

She flung off the sheet and rolled over. "It has been four whole days," she moaned. Four endless, broiling, nerve-racking days. And four balmy, wide-awake nights, the kind of nights that should have crickets and the scent of honeysuckle and…and…

Someone breathing beside you.

She sat straight up in bed and clapped her hand over her mouth. Well! Not "someone," exactly. Jericho Silver was not just "someone."

Ah, Madison O'Donnell. Just what is *he?*

She pulled the sheet over her head and shut her eyes again. She could not face another day of waiting and wondering and wishing…

The sharp clatter of horses' hooves sounded on the street below, and in an instant Maddie threw off the cover and streaked to the window.

Two men on horseback. She recognized Jericho's low-brimmed gray hat, but the second man, who was that? She pushed aside the curtain, shoved the sash up, and leaned out for a closer look.

The stranger's wrists were tied to the saddle horn, and his mount was roped to Jericho's mare. An outlaw! She leaned so far out the window she teetered on the sill and had to grab for the frame. Then she spied the bandanna around the man's neck, that strange shade of red-orange she'd seen at the mercantile. One of the Tucker gang.

Hurriedly she ducked back into the room, splashed her face with water from the china washbasin, and pulled on her shirtwaist and a skirt. Then she sped down the staircase and out onto the board walkway in front of the hotel. She had to race along the street to catch up with him.

"Jericho!"

He looked up. His face was pasty gray, his eyes unfocused with exhaustion.

He reined up in front of her. "Morning, Maddie." His heavy-lidded gaze traveled over her from head to toe and a baffled expression crossed his dust-streaked countenance.

Maddie looked down at her skirt. Had she put it on backward? No. And her one hastily donned petticoat did not show at the hem, so...? She dropped her eyes lower to examine her shoes.

She *had* no shoes. Mercy, had she really dashed out in public, in plain sight, with bare feet? She could not bring herself to meet Jericho's eyes. After a long moment she heard his low chuckle.

"Mighty pretty...mornin'," he murmured. He lifted his reins and moved on down the street toward the jail. Maddie raced up back to the hotel and up the stairs for her shoes.

Ten minutes later Jericho stepped onto the boardwalk beneath her hotel room window and looked up. Her heart skipped. She had been watching for him.

He tipped his head to one side, indicating the restaurant near the hotel. Checking to make sure she had shoes on her feet, she sped down the carpeted stairway, outside and down the street, and into the restaurant.

Without a word, Jericho took her elbow and guided her to their usual table, away from the window. He looked dreadful, hollow-eyed and rumpled, as if he had slept in his shirt for a week. At her inquiring look he shrugged, ran a hand over his dark-stubbled chin and sent her a crooked smile. She would bet he had not slept since she last saw him.

"Coffee, Rita," Jericho grated. "Pronto."

"Sure, Johnny. My stars, you look awful."

Maddie's thoughts exactly. "Jericho, are you all right?"

"I will be," he said heavily. He straddled the chair across from her and ran his hand—his right hand, she noted—through his tousled dark hair. "Right now, I'm damn tired."

And hungry, judging from the terse breakfast order he gave the waitress.

Rita glanced at Maddie. "And for you, Miz O'Donnell?"

Suddenly she was ravenous. "Steak and scrambled eggs, please. And lots of fried potatoes."

Once their breakfasts arrived, she watched Jericho's weary eyes scan the room before he focused on her.

"I nabbed one of them," he said some minutes later, frustration evident in his tired voice. "But that still leaves four more on the loose." He swallowed a gulp of coffee as their food arrived. "Next time..."

Maddie sat bolt upright. "Next time," she said crisply, "we try *my* plan."

"Don't think so, Maddie. I think I know where they're holed up for the time being. All I have to do is—"

She smacked her fork onto her plate so hard a slice of fried potato bounced out onto the tablecloth. She snatched it up between thumb and forefinger and waved it in front of him.

"Now you listen to me, Jericho Silver. You gave me your word." She popped the potato slice into her mouth and waited.

"Maddie, be sensible. I didn't come back empty-handed. I brought in one of the gang, but it wasn't easy. The others hightailed it off into the hills."

"Then it is time for *my* plan."

"No." He turned his chair around for better access to the platter of steak and fried eggs in front of him.

"But—"

"I said no, dammit. Hush up and let me eat."

"Jericho," she said, her tone sharp and hard as a steel ax. "You agreed you would try my plan next. I made that bargain with you in good faith, and you cannot wriggle out of it, you just can't. We shook hands on it, and I know what that means out here in the West."

He looked up. "Oh, yeah?" A low laugh rumbled from his throat. "What would a big-city girl like you know about life in the West?"

His tone was not challenging, exactly. Just determined. Well, she could be determined, too.

"All right, laugh. But I do know some things about the West. I know that a man's word is as good as his handshake. You told me so yourself."

"Must not have been thinking too clear," he muttered.

"You cannot pretend you are not an honorable man, can you? Of course not. Besides, how can you reject my plan before you know what it is? And besides that—"

Jericho groaned. "Okay, okay. Stop your yammering. Makes my head feel like the inside of a beehive."

Worse than a beehive. The woman could nag a man to distraction, could drive him to curse and drink and probably get into a mess of trouble just tryin' to stay one jump ahead of her.

When it came to Maddie, he figured he had to be *two* jumps ahead. She had a will as stiff as a green-oak limb and a mind like one of those woven willow traps the Nez Percé used for fishing: only one way in and no way out.

While she waited for him to say something, her cheeks grew pinker and pinker. Hell, she sure looked pretty.

"Well?" she said sharply.

Jericho laid his knife on his plate and began to twirl his empty coffee mug around and around on the tablecloth. He figured she'd explode with impatience if he didn't let her have her say.

"All right, Mrs. Detective, I'm listening."

"Very well, Mister Sheriff, I will tell you my plan."

She explained her idea in detail, watching his face.

He let her talk until she ran out of breath. "You talked Old Man Warriner at the bank into going along with this idea?"

"Yes, I did. He was not the least bit difficult to convince. Mr. Warriner saw the logic of my scheme in an instant."

"I'll bet," Jericho said in a dry voice. "Warriner's not known for his analytical mind."

"Well, he agreed it was a clever idea. He thought sending another fake shipment was…was a brilliant idea."

"Brilliant, huh?"

"That is what I said, Jericho. Are you not listening to me?" Probably not. She would bet the sheriff had already made up his mind and was just humoring her. That made her so furious she considered dumping her coffee over his head.

"Sure, I'm listenin'. Let's see, now. First we stir up a big hullabaloo about Warriner's fake gold shipment on the Portland train—"

"And we pretend it's heavily guarded," she interrupted.

"Okay. My posse and I—"

"And me! You cannot leave me behind." She would die if she missed the chance to help capture the outlaws. Her reputation as a Pinkerton agent depended on completing successful missions. Besides, an adventure would help keep her mind off…well, never mind. She sipped her coffee and waited.

He shot her a look that could spit bullets. "Yeah, I sure couldn't forget you," he grumbled. "So, we make sure everybody in town knows about the gold shipment, and I—"

"We," she interrupted.

"Yeah, 'we.' We get on the train and wait for the gang to show up. That right so far?"

Maddie shook her head. "No. The first time is just for show. The next time is when we make our move. We make another fake shipment and the gang hears about it and—"

"It'll never work, Maddie. The gang's holed up somewhere. Tucker will never know a shipment— even a fake one—is on its way."

"But of course he will," she snapped. "Whoever is tipping him off will ride to their camp and dangle the bait right in front of his nose."

Jericho sighed heavily. "Maddie, I'll—we'll— have to ride every train to Portland waiting for Tucker to strike."

"No, we will not, Jericho. You are not listening to me. We have to make only two trips. First we make a big fuss and fake one shipment, and then we tell everyone exactly when the next gold shipment is planned. Someone here in town will go off and alert Tucker about that shipment date, and then on the day of the supposed shipment we board the train and—"

"It's a waste of time. I could track them all the

way to Idaho in the time it'll take traveling back and forth between Smoke River and Portland."

"Jericho, you are the most stubborn man I have ever known. But you are also intelligent enough to recognize a good idea when you hear it, and this is a very good idea."

"Won't work, Mrs. Detective. I can see why Warriner liked your plan. It won't risk his gold. But it won't nab Tucker, either."

"Yes, it will! He is sure to rob the train, and we will be right there to arrest him."

"Nope. We already tried that. You got your leg skinned by a bullet."

She pinned him with eyes like flat green stones. "Jericho, you promised. You gave me your word."

He just stared at her over his coffee mug. It just might be a good idea to set a trap for Tucker and lie in wait on the train, but the risk to Maddie wasn't worth it. He didn't want her anywhere near the Tucker gang.

Besides, spending another night in Portland with her didn't seem the least bit intelligent. In fact, he thought with a twinge of regret, it would be downright foolhardy.

And damn dangerous.

But she was right—he had given his word, and not once since he was a kid had he ever gone back on it. He didn't like her idea, not one bit, but he had promised.

"Okay, Mrs. Detective, we'll try your plan."

He stood up slowly. "I'm going over to see Warriner at the bank."

She sprang up out of her chair. "I will go with you."

Jericho just shook his head. Being around Maddie was like trying to outrun a swarm of bees.

Being around Maddie was…driving him crazy. He couldn't stop thinking about kissing her that night at the boardinghouse. In fact, for the last four days it was *all* he could think about.

He'd never let her know that, though. Whatever fire he felt smoldering in his chest he'd have to damp down for good when she went back to Chicago. He sure as hell didn't want to get in so deep he couldn't walk away when the time came.

Chapter Fifteen

By suppertime, Jericho and Maddie had spread enough rumors that the whole town was talking about the supposed gold shipment the following morning on the seven-o'clock train to Portland.

By sunup the next day the townspeople gathered at the station to watch the bulky Wells Fargo bags being loaded into the mail car.

Maddie boarded, making a show of going to Portland "for some shopping." Dressmaker Verena Forester stood on the platform in a trim gray silk day dress calling last-minute instructions to her client.

"Not too heavy a wool, Mrs. O'Donnell. And be sure to purchase enough for a matching hat."

Maddie raised her voice theatrically. "I won't forget, Verena. Thank you for reminding me."

Jericho and his posse, Rooney Cloudman and Colonel Wash Halliday, bristling with sidearms, ostentatiously climbed on board, and with a lurch the train chugged off down the tracks. Unknown to the townspeople, the "posse" would debark at the first stop where they had horses waiting and be home in Smoke River in time for supper.

Maddie settled into her seat in the passenger car and swallowed a bite of the extra biscuits Rita had packed. The plan was perfect. Except...

She sat next to Jericho wondering when he would mention that kiss. What she should say.

But he didn't say one word about it. Perhaps his mind was on their plan. That thought brought a little hiccup to her thinking. "There's just one thing," she said hesitantly.

Jericho pulled his gaze away from the scene rolling by outside the window. "Yeah?"

"What if the gang really *does* show up today?"

"They won't. Their snitch in town hasn't had enough time to ride out to wherever Tucker's camp is now and tip them off. But they'll know for sure about our next fake shipment, and that's when they'll come runnin'."

And Jericho swore he'd be there to capture them. Without Maddie, if he could figure out how to manage it.

Maddie patted her mouth with a napkin. "I have been trying to identify who exactly is tipping Tucker off."

Jericho reached into the wicker basket for another biscuit. "Relax, Mrs. Detective. Whoever it is should be runnin' his horse into a lather right now, trying to reach Tucker. We're perfectly safe."

"Oh, good. Jericho, when we get to Portland,

could we…? I mean, I would so much like to visit Sundae again."

Jericho stared at her. "That palomino you fell in love with? Sure, I guess so."

And then another thought hit him and he sat straight up in his seat as if a ball of lightning had rolled onto his lap. *What happened after that?* She'd visit her horse, and then what? That left a whole evening, and another long night, alone with Maddie.

Under his shirt collar, Jericho began to sweat. He knew only one thing. No way in hell were they going to share a hotel room like they had before.

"Why, Mr. and Mrs. Silver," the hotel clerk said with a smile on his round, shiny face. "How nice to see you again."

Jericho opened his mouth to explain, but the man plunged on. "Good time to visit, folks, it being Fourth of July and all. City's got lotsa things planned, big picnic and a band concert, fireworks in the evening, and—"

"We would like two separate rooms," Maddie interrupted.

"How's that again? *Two* rooms?" The clerk's wiry red eyebrows went up, then settled into a frown. "Oh, I see," he said, leaning toward Jericho. "Little lady's upset, is she?"

"No, the 'little lady' is not upset," Maddie said through clenched teeth. "It's just that we are not really—"

"Don't make no nevermind, Mrs. Silver. Hotels

are all full up anyway. Every hotel in town's busting its seams, so it's one room or noth—"

"Fine," Jericho interrupted. "Let's have the key."

Maddie followed him up the carpeted staircase with an odd sense of elation. She knew it was purely scandalous to share a room with the sheriff again, but no one would ever know.

Besides, at the moment she did not care. She was hot and stiff from sitting on the train for six long hours, and what she cared about at this moment was having a bath and a big steak dinner.

After all, they had shared a room the last time they were in Portland. This would be no different.

Oh, yes, it would.

The last time they were in Portland was before Jericho had kissed her. Whether he remembered doing so or not did not matter; that kiss had changed things between them. She knew it as surely as cats had kittens. And he knew it, too. She could tell by the way he avoided her eyes.

Jericho unlocked the hotel room door and she stepped inside. Heavens, it was the same room they had shared before. The same window overlooking the street below, the same washstand, the same two beds, but now, oh, heavens! The beds had been shoved together in the center of the room.

"You want a bath brought up?"

"What? Oh, a bath. Yes, I would like a bath." But good gracious, she could not bathe with him in the room.

"Jericho, do you not have something you need to do in Portland?"

His dark eyebrows rose, but his mouth twitched. "Do?"

"Yes, 'do.' You know, visit the livery stable or the mercantile or…something."

"Nope," he said with a grin. "Can't think of a thing."

"But, well, then could you—"

"Oh, sure. I'll order a bath for you on my way out."

He laughed on his way to the door.

Unless she was very much mistaken, he had been teasing her. Imagine, short-spoken, no-nonsense Sheriff Silver with a sense of humor.

"Where are you going?"

"Barber shop next door to the hotel."

"Jericho?"

He still would not meet her gaze. "Yeah?"

"After supper, could I…could we…visit Sundae?"

Jericho had to laugh. Here they were, holed up together in a compromising situation, and she wanted to visit a horse? As long as he lived, he'd never understand this woman.

"Could we?" she persisted.

He did look at her, then. Straight into her clear green eyes, and the longing he saw in their depths made his gut clench. "We can sure as hell try, Maddie."

All the way down the stairs he shook his head in disbelief. Guess it was plain damn stupid of him to worry about sharing a room with Mrs. Detective; she was more interested in a palomino mare than she was in him.

After supper in the hotel dining room, they set out on foot for the carnival grounds where the Fourth of July fireworks display would be held. The horse corral would be in the field next to the grounds.

The evening was balmy, the stars overhead like tiny diamonds tossed at random across the purple-black night sky. Jericho inhaled the spicy-sweet scent of roses and felt a dart of pain under his breastbone. Little Bear had loved the roses in the orphanage garden. He wondered if they were still there.

Instantly he clamped his teeth together. That place held nothing but bad memories and the feeling of loneliness and not belonging that he'd tried to shake for twenty years. No way in hell did he want to see the place, or its rose garden, ever again.

In silence he kept pace with Maddie along streets lined with stately homes behind intricate black wrought-iron fences. They walked four blocks in silence before Maddie spoke.

"These houses remind me of where I grew up."

"Pretty fancy," Jericho commented.

"Oh, not so fancy inside. Our house had only five bedrooms."

Jericho said nothing. Jupiter, only five bedrooms? The difference between his life and Maddie's was like tumbleweeds in a fancy room with velvet drapes.

He tried to think of something else, but all kinds

of thoughts kept bumping their ugly heads into his brain. Five bedrooms!

Ah, hell, maybe he shouldn't think so much.

He liked this woman. He liked her better than he'd liked any female he'd ever known, except maybe for Little Bear.

"Jericho? The orphanage you were raised in was here in Portland, was it not?"

"Yeah," he said shortly.

"What was it like, really?"

His belly tightened. "Strict," he shot back. "Cold. Bad food. As different from houses like these—" he gestured at the huge brick mansion they were passing "—as potatoes from ripe peaches." He didn't want to go on.

"You were not happy there?"

"Not one damn day."

"I was not happy in my father and mother's house, either."

That surprised him. She'd probably had everything a kid could want, friends, music lessons, parties.

"Really," he said drily.

"Really," she echoed. She hesitated. "I was... lonely."

Oh, sure she was. The poor little rich girl with too many dresses. They moved on without talking until he heard her voice again.

"Jericho, you did not like me when I came to Smoke River, did you?"

"You're right, I didn't." He couldn't think of another word to add, so he snapped his jaw shut and kept walking.

"But we've been through a terrible ordeal together, both of us getting shot, I mean."

"Yeah, what of it?"

"Then we are friends now, are we not?"

His throat closed. Friends? He'd tried hard not to think too much about their relationship, but he knew damn well they were more than friends. How much more, he couldn't bring himself to consider.

"Yeah, I guess we're friends."

She gave a little skip, which made him laugh. "You cannot imagine how glad that makes me."

"Why?" He almost choked on the question.

"Well, I...I think quite highly of you."

"I think highly of you, too, Maddie." He kept his voice steady, but his insides were flipping like Mexican jumping beans.

She scooted out in front and spun to face him. "You do? Really?" She walked backward until she came to a dip in the sidewalk and her balance wavered. He snaked a hand to her shoulder to steady her.

Abruptly she halted. Barely conscious of what he was doing, Jericho closed his fingers on her other shoulder. She smiled up at him.

For the first time in a bunch of hours he let himself look directly into her eyes. Big mistake. He wanted to pull her close, wrap his arms around her and hold on. Wanted to feel her heart hammer against his.

What the hell was the matter with him?

He blew out a lungful of air. Nothing was the matter. He simply wanted to kiss her. He was a man and she was a woman and he wanted to kiss her. He wanted to close his eyes and breathe in her lavender scent, let it sweep him off to that muddled, happy state he remembered from when he'd kissed her before.

"Maddie..."

"Oh, look! There's the gypsy fortune-teller! The horse corral is right behind her tent. Come on." She grabbed his hand and tugged him past the gaudy canvas, and then she stopped dead. What had been the horse corral was nothing but an empty field with a split-rail fence running around it.

"They're gone," she moaned. "The horses are gone. Sundae is gone."

She stood staring at the space, shaking her head in disbelief. "Sundae is gone," she said again. This time her voice broke.

His stomach turned over. "Probably some rancher from hereabouts had loaned his stock to the carnival folks and..."

She nodded and sniffled back tears. "Of course. I sh-should have thought of that, but truly I did not w-want to."

Damn. He'd give anything if she wouldn't cry; it did funny things to his insides.

"Maddie, look, the ice-cream stand's still there. Want an ice-cream cone?"

"Y-yes," she said slowly. "No. Oh, I don't know."

He took her hand and drew her to the ice-cream

vendor's stall. She stood in front of the man for a long time and finally ordered a double strawberry cone.

He couldn't watch her lick it. Her little pink tongue flicking in and out gave him the worst hard-on he'd had in years.

All the way back to the hotel he struggled to keep his eyes on the sidewalk and not on her mouth, and when she finally crunched up the last of the crisp wafer he let out a sigh of relief.

Then he spent eight blocks trying like hell not to notice the smear of pink ice cream on her lower lip.

He groaned out loud. Sleeping in the same room with Maddie was the worst idea he'd ever had in his life.

He wanted to touch her so bad he ached.

Chapter Sixteen

The instant Jericho puffed out the lantern on his nightstand, Maddie stripped down to her camisole and petticoats and crawled between the cool sheets. She heard Jericho thump off his boots and maybe his shirt and jeans; she could not be sure in the dark, and anyway, she knew she should not be paying attention to what clothes he had on. Or off.

Her body felt heavy and an ache was beginning behind her eyes. She rolled onto her side, then flopped onto her other side and closed her eyes. Or tried to. Her lids kept popping open every time Jericho stirred.

Why was she not sleeping? Oh, what did it matter? He lay quietly, as if he hadn't a care in the world, while she felt more restless and keyed up than she had since she was a girl performing at one of her piano recitals.

This was not like the excitement of starting a new assignment for Mr. Pinkerton, or even the bubbly pride she felt after successfully bringing in evidence for the capture of a wanted man. Her brain told her everything was going well; her nerves were signaling something else. Nothing was working out as she'd expected.

Her beautiful mare, Sundae, was gone and Jericho was being impossible. Clearly he did not want her along on this mission—or any mission. She felt useless and confused and not valued.

She didn't belong out here in the West. She didn't understand the blunt speech, the brusque manners, the rough-and-tumble ways of everyone she came in contact with. Even Mr. Warriner at the bank had treated her with polite disregard. She'd had to pound her gloved fist on his desk to get him to listen to her ideas.

Why, *why* had Mr. Pinkerton sent her out here to this godforsaken part of the country? He'd said he wanted to "broaden her experience," but he must have known she wouldn't fit in, not in a million years. Except for that lovely palomino horse she'd befriended, not one living creature out here cared about her.

Even Jericho. That kiss he'd given her had meant nothing. He hadn't mentioned it. Maybe he didn't even remember it. True, he had been burning with fever at the time, but even so, sheriffs did not kiss their agents every day of the week. Or did they? Maybe this sheriff did and then just forgot about it. About her.

And that hurt!

She flipped over onto her other side and tried to think clearly. Could this uneasiness be because of that maddening man in the next bed?

The edgy fluttering inside her was unbearable. She slipped out from under the sheet, draped the quilt around her bare shoulders, and tiptoed to the window.

It was long past midnight; the entire city was asleep.

Nothing moved on the street below, and only shadows marked the building entrances. All at once she wanted to smell the clean, fresh air outside.

Releasing the catch lock, she quietly slid the sash up until the warm night air wafted against her face. Somewhere near the hotel a town clock tolled three times and then fell silent.

She wedged her hip onto the windowsill and leaned out, drinking in the scent of roses from the city park on the next corner. Above her, millions of stars shone in a sky so black it looked like crushed velvet. It was so vast and beautiful it made her want to cry. The whole world was asleep but for her.

"Maddie?" a raspy voice spoke from the bed behind her. "What are you doing sitting in the window?"

"Just…thinking about things."

"What things?" He sounded wide-awake now.

Before she could answer he was standing behind her, so close she could feel the warmth of his body. "What things?" he repeated.

"Oh, odd things. Like why I am feeling empty inside when I ate a big steak for supper and a strawberry ice-cream cone before bed."

"Maybe you're still hungry?"

She ignored the question. She was hungry, but not for food. The hollow sensation yawning in her belly was for something else entirely. Something she was afraid to admit to herself.

"Just look, Jericho. The stars are so far away, so beautiful. They make me think about…about things I don't want to think about." About how lonely her life was, despite the excitement of life in Chicago, despite even her adventurous missions for Mr. Pinkerton.

He said nothing.

"Jericho, do you ever wonder what life is really all about?"

"Yeah, I do."

"I wonder, too. Right now I wonder what my own life is all about."

He gave a soft laugh. "You're a good detective, Maddie. How come you haven't figured that out?"

"I do not know," she said on a sigh. "I wonder sometimes if being a detective is enough to make my existence matter."

She tipped her head up to gaze at the stars. "We are such tiny insignificant beings, really. What difference could one little life make?"

His voice was suddenly low and tense. "You think like this a lot?"

She flinched as if he had poked at her spine. "No. I have never thought about these things before."

"Why tonight, Maddie? Maybe it has something to do with finding out that Sundae was gone?"

"Oh." She said nothing for a full minute, and then she swiped her palm across her cheeks.

Jericho stepped in close and touched her shoulder.

Maddie gave a little hiccup and turned her face into his chest. "I know she's just a horse, but she was so strong and beautiful and she, well, she seemed to like me."

Her cheek was wet against his skin, but he didn't give a damn.

"Oh, it isn't about Sundae, I guess." She sniffled. "It's— I don't know what it is. The stars, maybe."

Jericho drew in a soft breath. "Yeah, maybe. I know how they make *me* feel."

"How?" Her voice sounded wobbly.

"Lonely," he answered after a long moment. "I've never said that to anybody before." He swallowed and looked away. Watching her trying not to cry made him hurt inside.

Without thinking, he wrapped his arms around her. Big mistake. The feel of her frame trembling against his drove the last sensible thought from his head. He bent and found her mouth.

For an instant she went absolutely still, and then she reached up to fold her arms about his neck. God help him, he'd never felt anything so wonderful in his entire life.

Her lips moved under his and he tasted salty tears and strawberries. He broke away, gulped a breath, and kissed her again. This time she kissed him back, tentative at first, almost shy, and then with an intensity that sent his brain reeling.

When she moaned, he lifted his head. "I've

waited days and days for you to kiss me again," she whispered.

Jericho closed his eyes. "Wish I'd known. Wouldn't have waited so long."

"Yes, you would," she said with a choked laugh. "One thing I have learned about you, Sheriff, is that you think things through before you make a move."

A chuckle rumbled out of his throat. "Just cautious, I guess."

"Oh, no, Jericho. I would bet anything it is not caution. It is fear."

He gave an involuntary jerk, then tightened his arms around her. "You talk too much, Maddie."

He could tell her corset was unlaced, and that top thing she wore over it was loose as well. Then there were all those petticoats...

Wait just a damn minute. What was he thinking?

He wanted her. Hell, yes, he wanted her. But dammit, he wasn't going to send her back to Chicago with his heart in her pocket.

His arms dropped away.

"Jericho?"

"Time for bed." He drew in an uneven breath. "Alone."

"Jericho, stay with me. Please. Just stay beside me."

"Jeez, Maddie, I—" He still had on his jeans, but so what? Probably safer that way.

He drew her over to her bed, pressed her down, and pulled the sheet and the quilt up over her body. Swallowing a groan, he stretched out beside her on top of the quilt and prayed his erection would ease off. He considered stripping down to his drawers but something stayed his hand. Too dangerous. Instead, he rolled toward her and nestled her head against his shoulder.

Her hair felt like a flutter of silk against his skin. He wanted to weave his fingers through it and kiss her some more. A lot more. Hell, he hadn't felt this alive, or this scared, since he was a kid at the orphanage.

He tried like anything to shut down his brain. What was he scared of?

You're scared she'll leave, you idiot.

Well, hell, she was planning to do just that as soon as she finished this assignment. He closed his eyes and tried not to think about it.

But he couldn't stop remembering things—the steely look on her face when confronting that robber in the mail car, the stubborn stiffening of her spine after he'd ordered her back to town when he'd ridden out to find Tucker's camp, the sparkle in her eyes when she first rode Sundae. And, oh, hell, the bleakness last night when she'd found the mare gone.

He swallowed a groan. He'd made a big mistake with Maddie O'Donnell. He'd let her slip under his skin when he wasn't looking, let himself kiss her soft mouth and touch her skin. Now he wondered if he'd ever be free of her.

Yeah, well, he had to let it go. If he was going to live safe, protect himself like he'd always done, he had to stop thinking about her. Had to stop wanting her.

He let his eyelids close.

The next thing he knew it was morning and Maddie was gone.

He found her at breakfast. She was all business, as if last night had never happened. Hell, maybe he'd dreamed it.

She plunked her coffee cup down and met his gaze. "When we return to Smoke River we must make sure Mr. Warriner at the bank is still amenable to my plan. Then tomorrow we can…"

Jericho listened as she rattled on. Sitting across from her, drinking his morning coffee, he wondered how he'd gotten through the night. He hadn't slept much, and now his thoughts were making fuzzy disconnected circles in his brain.

Finally, he plunked down his coffee cup. "Your idea might work, Maddie. But that's not what we're going to do."

When she opened her mouth to protest he cut her off with a sharp gesture. "I've made a decision, and that's that."

"But why? We agreed to be partners, and now when things—"

"Be quiet, Maddie. Unless you want me to climb over this table and kiss you silly in front of everybody, just keep your mouth shut and go on eating your breakfast."

She looked so completely poleaxed he wanted to

laugh. She blushed crimson although kept on forking in her eggs and fried potatoes, but she ate so slowly they almost missed the train back to Smoke River.

Maddie gazed out the train window as the locomotive chuffed slowly into Smoke River. It was actually a pretty little town. Leafy green trees shaded the narrow streets. Every front yard had a garden chock-full of scarlet zinnias or yellow daisies, and honeysuckle vines rambled up porch posts and across verandas. Two little girls in blue gingham pinafores playing hopscotch in front of the church turned to wave at the train.

She bit her lower lip. But it was such a *little* town. Only one mercantile, a one-room schoolhouse, only one hotel and a single dressmaker. No opera house. No libraries or fine restaurants or museums or art galleries. What did people *do* in an out-of-the-way place like this?

Life here would be twice as boring as being trapped in a city marriage.

The locomotive tooted one long blast and steamed into the station. They disembarked onto the empty platform, and Jericho grabbed up her small satchel.

"I'll walk you to the hotel. Then I have to check the jail and talk to Sandy."

Maddie studied his face. A hot flare of something showed in his eyes, followed by a look of resignation.

"I'll meet you in the restaurant for supper," he said.

"You must be tired of eating all your meals with me, Sheriff."

"Nope. Meet me," he ordered. "There's something I need to tell you."

Her heart flipped up and over. "What is it?"

"You'll find out, Maddie. Just hold your horses. I'll see you in an hour."

It wasn't a question, it was an order. Maddie's spine stiffened. Jericho had no right to order her around. Kissing her last night gave him no control over…anything. They were equals. Partners. A team.

"I will thank you not to give me orders as if I were a servant," she said crisply.

He said not one word all the way to the hotel, and by the time they reached the door to her room, Maddie's annoyance had bloomed into anger.

"Did you hear what I said?"

He scowled and dropped her satchel just inside the door. "You're not a servant, Maddie, and you know it. But someone has to make sensible decisions, and today it's gonna be me."

She tried to shut the door in his face but he blocked it with one booted foot, touched two fingers to his hat brim and gave her a lopsided grin. Then he tramped back down the staircase.

She waited five minutes then slipped down the stairs herself and went about her own set of errands. She made good use of the time, and within the hour, she marched into the restaurant armed with new information.

Jericho was waiting for her at the corner table. His lean tanned face looked tight, and his eyes would not meet hers. With Jericho, that was a bad sign.

He stood up as she approached. He might have hated the orphanage, but the nuns had surely taught him good manners.

She settled into the chair opposite him and smiled at Rita, who hovered nearby. "Coffee, please." She glanced at Jericho's half-empty cup. "With brandy."

The waitress's eyes were sharply perceptive. "Musta been a tough trip, Miz O'Donnell. Johnny's on his third cup."

He was, was he? She guessed he needed some Dutch courage for what he wanted to tell her. Instinctively she knew it was something she would not want to hear.

"Is everything all right at the jail?" she ventured.

"Yeah. Prisoner's complaining about Sandy's coffee. Name's Roscoe Dipley and he's one son-of-a-miserable-no-count creature if I ever saw one. Keeps bragging how his friends are gonna bust him out of jail."

Maddie caught her breath. "Could they really do that?"

"They could try, but nobody's gonna bust him free without taking a bellyful of lead. Sandy's a crack shot."

"And you would be there, as well. Your wrist has healed nicely."

"Yeah, it has. But I won't be there."

Here it comes, she thought. *And he knows I will not like it. That is why he won't look at me.* She gulped down a swallow of her brandy-laced coffee.

"Maddie, I've been thinking…"

"That's your problem, Jericho. You think too much."

His eyes flashed a darker blue. "I don't call it 'thinking too much.' I call it planning ahead."

"And what is it we are planning, Sheriff?"

"*We* are not planning anything. *I'm* riding out in the morning with Colonel Halliday and Rooney Cloudman. We're gonna surprise the Tucker gang in their hideout."

"But…but I thought you always worked alone?"

"Not this time. I want this over and done with. Now. The way to do that is…well, to use help. Professional help," he added.

She clenched her fist in her lap. "You said we would try my plan next. My plan," she said, narrowing her eyes, "is not yet finished."

"It *is* finished," he said flatly.

"It is *not* finished." Her voice rose half an octave. "The next step is when we board the train again and capture—"

"It's no good, Maddie." He raked his fingers through his dark hair.

"Why not? It was good before!" She knew her voice was getting louder, but she didn't care.

"Things are different now," he growled.

"What things? Our plan was to fake the gold—"

"Dammit, keep your voice down. You want the whole town to know?"

Maddie bit her lip and stared out the front window to get herself under control. It was getting dark outside, she noted. And she was getting hungry.

"Jericho," she said in as patient a voice as she could manage. "We need to capture the Tucker gang. We can do that if we take the train to Portland tomorrow morning and—"

"No, we can't." A muscle twitched under his eye. "We're not gonna do that. And we're not gonna jaw about it. Rita?" He signaled the waitress. "Bring us a couple of steaks."

Rita grinned. "How—"

"Rare," he snapped.

"Miz O'Donnell?"

Maddie glowered at Jericho. "Rare. And more coffee, just like the last cup, please, only more brandy."

They waited in icy silence until their dinners arrived, and for the next half hour the only sounds were the clink of silverware and the tink of cups on china saucers.

Maddie swallowed the last of her liquor-laced coffee and noticed a pleasant warmth spreading through her chest. She was still furious with him, but she knew enough to keep quiet until they were alone.

Jericho ordered a fourth refill on his coffee and she ground her teeth in impatience. Finally, *finally,* he ushered her out into the warm, softly scented air of what should have been a pleasant summer evening.

"Jericho—"

"Not now, Maddie." He walked her all the way to her hotel room without speaking.

"You had better come in," she said, clipping off each word, "so we can straighten out this misunderstanding."

Jericho did not answer, just strode into her room and slammed the door behind him.

Maddie pinned him with hard green eyes. "I spoke with Mr. Warriner at the bank earlier this afternoon. Our original plan is in place, and tomorrow morning the train leaves at seven o'clock."

"The hell it does!" Jericho exploded.

"It most certainly does," Maddie shouted in his face. "Jericho Silver, what has gotten into you all of a sudden?" She turned away to light the lamp on the dresser but he caught her arm. He was so mad he couldn't say a damn thing for a full minute.

"Well?" she shouted. Instantly she clapped her hand over her mouth. "Good heavens, I never shout. In all my life I cannot remember ever raising my voice like this to anyone."

Jericho had never before felt such pure, uncomplicated rage. "What's gotten into me? *You* are what's gotten into me, Maddie! I don't want to— I can't risk— Oh, the hell with it."

He pulled her into his arms and kissed her, hard. She pummeled his chest with her fists, but he kept kissing her and gradually she quieted.

But she didn't pull away.

"Maddie," he said when he could breathe again. "I can't put you in danger."

Even in the dark he could see the way her eyes blazed. "Why, you great big liar!" But her voice was different, softer than he'd ever heard it. "Feeling responsible for me is only half the reason," she continued. "The other half is… Oh, my, I do not think I can say this."

"The other half is that I…" His voice turned hoarse. "I said it before. I can't stand knowing you might get hurt. I care about that, Maddie. A lot."

That was only half true. The truth was he cared about *her.* "Maddie, please. I've got to go with Wash and Rooney tomorrow morning. I've got to."

She said nothing, but a sparkling drop of moisture clung to her dark lashes, and that did him in.

"Maddie." He scooped her up into his arms, laid her on the bed and followed her down. He wanted to hold her tight against him, wanted to touch her. He caught her mouth under his and moved over her lips until he couldn't think straight.

When he lifted his head, she stared up at him. "I have just one thing to say, Jericho Silver."

"Yeah? Say it."

"You think a kiss is going to change my mind, do you not?"

"Oh, hell, Maddie. It was more than just a kiss, and you know it."

He kissed her forehead, her throat, the soft place behind her ear, and gradually her breathing steadied and then slowed. His own was getting hard to control.

"Maddie, we're gonna be in trouble if you don't tell me to stop."

"I do not want you to stop," she murmured. "I want this to go on forever."

Chapter Seventeen

"Maddie," Jericho breathed. "You sure you really want this?"

He knew what *he* wanted. He'd wanted it ever since she walked off that train and into his life. But he had a job to do. Now he was facing two jobs—bringing in the Tucker gang and keeping Maddie safe.

Just enough moonlight filtered through the muslin curtains to illuminate her face. She was smiling, and her answer rocked him down to his toes.

"Jericho, take off your gun belt."

He rolled away from her to wrestle the metal tongue free, then slid the sheathed revolvers onto the floor beside the bed.

"And your boots," she whispered.

When they thumped onto the carpet next to his sidearms she gave a half-swallowed sigh and rose up to kiss one side of his mouth. The brush of her lips felt like a butterfly landing near his chin.

"Now take off everything else."

Jericho blinked. For a minute he wasn't sure he'd heard right. This was Mrs. Detective, Maddie O'Donnell? Hell, he'd wanted to see her naked a hundred times, but he'd never dreamed she would want...

He stood and stripped to his drawers.

"Everything," she reminded.

"Now you, Maddie." His voice was so thick it was hard to get the words out.

She sighed again. "I want you to do it."

He laughed out loud. Maddie had to be the most unusual woman in the entire territory.

"Maddie," he whispered against her ear. "Are you sure about this? Because if you're not—"

She gave him a lazy smile. "Oh, yes, I am sure. I have been sure ever since you first kissed me that night at the boardinghouse."

Jericho could think of nothing to say. Ever since then, he'd thought more about that kiss than he'd thought about getting enough to eat.

"I was beginning to think you were never going to kiss me again after that first time," she breathed. "I thought perhaps you did not remember it."

"Didn't think I had the right to kiss you again." He slipped the top button of her blouse free. "But that didn't stop the wanting."

Her skin was like warm silk. He wanted to touch her all over. He freed three more of the tiny buttons and spread the soft fabric open to press his mouth against her bare flesh. He kissed her all the way down to the lacy neckline of her camisole.

Her breathing checked and then he felt her hands on his bare chest. The hard swelling between his thighs began to ache.

Think of something else before you lose control and make a complete fool of yourself.

"Funny what kissing someone does," he murmured. "Afterward you can say things you might have thought about before but you never had the guts to say." He undid another button and loosened the ribbon of her camisole.

"Take this off," he said hoarsely. "Before I rip it."

She sat up, fiddled with buttonholes and ribbons and hooks, then petticoats and a bustle contraption tied around her waist. Shoes. Stockings. When a man was as hungry as he was, undressing a woman was way too slow. He wanted to tear everything away and bury his face against her flesh.

She stretched out beside him and slowly raised her arms over her head. With a groan, Jericho took one peaked nipple into his mouth.

"Yes," she whispered. "Oh, yes."

He could tell she was smiling; her voice sounded so…happy. Well, hell, he was smiling, too. They were both crazy as loons to be doing this. But he didn't feel crazy; he felt very sure. And, dammit, very scared.

Her entire silk-soft body smelled of lavender. Her breasts, everywhere he put his mouth, or his tongue, or both, tasted sweet, like ripe peaches. He shook his head at the thought. From now on, peaches would be his favorite fruit.

He smoothed his palm up one bare thigh, wove his fingers through the silky hair at her apex and heard her breath hiss in. Hell, he couldn't hold on much longer. He dipped one finger into her center and she cried out.

"Jericho," she moaned. "That feels wonderful. *You* are wonderful. Don't stop. Please don't stop."

Maddie heard herself cry out and her breath caught in surprise. She had never felt like this before, so free and floaty, and happy—ridiculously, gloriously happy. He was touching her. *Touching her.* She moved convulsively under his hand. She wanted to sing and laugh and weep, all at the same time.

Jericho's lean, hard body lifted over her and then his weight pressed against her everywhere. She felt him slide into her and then withdraw, then enter her again. And again.

Her hands closed into fists and she lifted her face and found her mouth open wide against his shoulder. His motions were slow and controlled and he didn't stop moving, even when she began to moan. Something built inside her until her body suddenly clenched and the darkness behind her eyelids exploded into a shower of stars.

His raspy breathing grew more and more uneven until all at once he stilled. With a shout he pulled out of her and spilled himself onto the quilt.

"I didn't want to do that," he confessed. "I wanted to bury myself inside you and just let it happen."

She reached up and wrapped her arms around

him. "I would have liked that, Jericho. Why didn't you?"

He raised himself up on his elbows and looked down into her face, still breathing hard. "Think a minute, Maddie. It's the only responsible thing I could do. I don't want to send you back to Chicago with a baby in your belly."

She tightened her arms across his muscled back and remained quiet for a long time. She had not thought beyond this moment, not considered possible consequences. Madison O'Donnell, who prided herself on always assessing consequences, had lost her head and followed blindly where her heart had led her, had tumbled into bed with a man for the first time since she was widowed.

What is happening to me?

Jericho rolled away and pulled her close. "Maddie..." He started to say something, but she laid a finger against his mouth. In a heartbeat he was asleep.

She tipped her head to study his face. His dark lashes were longer than they looked when he was awake and the beginning of a beard shadowed his chin. Squint lines radiated from the corners of his eyes, and his mouth...

A white-hot bolt of desire stabbed below her belly. His lips, his well-shaped mouth, made her want him all over again.

Jericho was not just any man; Jericho was extraordinary, unlike anyone she had ever known. He was so unusual she could scarcely believe he was real.

She smoothed back the black hair tangled over

his forehead and noticed that her fingers were trembling. She would not allow herself to think about him riding away in the morning. She was glad for this night with him. She would remember it the rest of her life.

Someone was banging on the hotel-room door. "Miz O'Donnell? *Miz O'Donnell!*"

Maddie sat up. "Yes? Who is it?"

"It's me, Sandy. I've gotta find the sheriff right away. The Tucker gang is robbing the bank!"

"Now? In the middle of the night?"

"Yes, ma'am. You know where the sheriff is?"

Jericho was already out of bed and into his jeans and gun belt. He yanked open the door and confronted his deputy.

"What's happened, Sandy?"

Sandy's mouth gaped open. "Well, I…" The boy turned beet-red. "You know Rita, the waitress at the restaurant? She woke me up pounding on the jailhouse door, screamin' about somethin' she saw on her way home from the restaurant after her shift."

"What," Jericho said as patiently as he could, "was it she saw?"

"Well…" The kid looked down at the floor. "Sheriff, you don't have your boots—"

"Sandy!"

"Oh, yeah. Rita saw four men on foot, leadin' their horses down Main Street."

"So?"

"Well, Old Man Warriner was stumblin' along

out in front of 'em, lookin' like he's seein' a ghost or somethin'. He had a revolver stickin' in his back."

Damn. They were going to force Warriner to open the safe. "Sandy, guard the jail. Might be they're also gonna try to break Dipley out."

"Yessir, Sheriff." He beat a fast retreat down the staircase and Jericho scrabbled under the bed for his boots.

"Maddie, I want you to stay here."

"There are four of them, Jericho. Only one of you."

"Do what I say," he ordered.

"But—"

He threw on his shirt, ran his fingers through his hair, then turned to her and grasped her shoulders. "Don't argue."

He kissed her. Then he kissed her again, harder. "And for God's sake, stay out of sight."

Once outside the hotel, Jericho raced down the shadowy street toward the brick building on the corner across from Ness's mercantile.

The bank looked dark and deserted. No light showed through the window of Warriner's office, where the safe was located. Probably black as a coal mine inside. There was no sign of anyone outside.

As he approached, he worked out a plan.

He scouted the perimeter of the building. Sure enough, behind the mercantile he found four horses tied to an elm tree. He recognized two of the animals as part of the Tucker string.

Damn fools. They expected to escape on foot with

the Wells Fargo sacks? That made no sense. One of the outlaws would have to bring the animals around at a signal from inside.

Jericho crouched, laid one hand on the closest animal and waited for someone to challenge him. Not a whisper. Quickly he untied the reins and ran them off one by one with a slap to the rump. Tucker wouldn't hear the noise from inside the bank.

Then he crept around the corner to the bank entrance and quietly inched the heavy oak door open. He was perfectly positioned to surprise them.

The interior was as dark as a mine shaft. With one hand on the wall and the other on his Colt, he moved to the iron-latticed teller's window and slid on through the turnstile. Now a faint light showed beneath the door to Warriner's office.

A voice drifted from behind the door, followed by an odd muffled *whump*. Then another. Making no sound, Jericho moved to the door and pressed his ear against the wood. More voices and a man's throaty laugh. Tucker.

Very carefully he laid his hand on the brass doorknob and began to twist it to the right. When it would turn no farther, he edged the door open a crack.

The first thing he saw was Old Man Warriner, a red-orange bandanna stuffed in his mouth. The graying banker was sitting on the floor by his big walnut desk, his wrists tied in front of him. He wore what looked like his nightshirt stuffed into brown gabardine trousers; looked as though the gang had rousted him out of bed. A tiny kerosene lantern threw weak light onto his puffy face. His eyes were wild with fright.

He'd have to be careful. Warriner didn't deserve to get hurt.

He pushed the door a scant inch wider. Four men, Tucker and three others, were wrestling open the heavy safe door. Scorched chair cushions were tossed into the corner. That explained the noise he'd heard; when Warriner refused to open the safe they must have shot off the combination lock, using the cushions to muffle the sound.

"That's far enough, Rafe." Tucker bent, lifted the lamp and peered inside. "There it is. Four of them big Wells Fargo bags of gold. Lefty, you go get the horses. We'll lug the gold sacks out and load 'em."

A skinny man Jericho recognized started for the door. Jericho drew his other revolver and kicked the door wide open.

"Hands in the air!"

Tucker made a move toward his sidearm, and Jericho sent a bullet through the holster hanging on his hip. He didn't want to kill him; he wanted the gang to stand trial.

"Drop your gun belts," he ordered. The men unbuckled and let their weapons drop to the floor. All but Tucker.

"Hell if I will," the outlaw growled.

"Hell if you won't." Jericho sent a well-placed slug into the man's upper arm, then flicked a look at Warriner.

"You okay, Sol?"

The banker nodded and held up his bound wrists. "Now, gentlemen, you're under ar—"

Tucker suddenly swept his boot against the lamp, and the room went black. Jericho couldn't see a damn thing. Scrabbling sounds came from the vault, and he figured the gang was hefting the canvas bags to their shoulders, using the darkness as cover.

He ducked back, using the door as a shield, and sent a shot over their heads. "Drop the bags," he ordered.

Two loud clunks sounded. That left two men still loading up. He crouched in position and peered around the door, desperately trying to see movement, shadows, anything that would tell him who was where.

Too late. A shot zinged past his shoulder and two more thudded into the wood plank door at his left. But the flashes from the fired weapons revealed their positions.

"Sol," Jericho yelled. "Lie flat." He heard the banker slide his bulk onto the floor.

He aimed at the paunchy outlaw closest to the door, and fired a bullet at knee height. A high cry and a thump told him the man was down. But Tucker was still armed, and from the scratching sounds Jericho figured the others were scrambling for their gun belts.

A sickening realization swept over him. He had his two Colts. They probably had six, maybe eight revolvers between them. Any second they'd start spraying bullets all over him. If he stood up, he wouldn't stand a chance. All the same, he wished like hell he could get to their weapons first.

Then from somewhere behind him a rifle cracked. What the devil— He'd ordered Sandy to stay at the jail, but for once in his life he was glad his deputy hadn't obeyed. Jericho flattened himself on the floor.

The shot was high enough to miss his head but just the right height to smack into the shoulder of someone standing. A shouted curse told him he was right.

Another rifle shot skimmed past his prone body and into the blackness. This one zinged against something metal—the safe, he guessed.

"Sheriff," a raspy voice whispered. "It's getting light. Draw them outside."

Sandy. He elbowed himself sideways until he was protected behind the open door.

Sandy stopped firing.

And so did Tucker's men. No sound came from the office except for the heavy breathing of the one he'd nailed earlier and the guttural cursing of the man Sandy had apparently hit in the shoulder.

Jericho waited in silence while sweat ran down his neck. A rustling sound told him his deputy had backed out of the bank foyer and was waiting for the gang to emerge. If he lay here long enough, the gray light of dawn would illuminate the single window in Warriner's office and he could see where to aim.

But then so could they. The gang was trapped inside, but the minute it was light enough they'd retrieve their guns.

No good. "Sandy?" he whispered. "Move outside."

No answer. Smart boy. Sandy was already outside, waiting. When the gang broke for an escape, they'd be caught in the crossfire—Jericho at their backs, Sandy in the street, facing them.

He drew in a deep breath and prepared to wait it out.

It didn't take long. The light filtering through the window went from gray to peach-pink. When it started to turn gold, the gang members made a run for it.

Afraid he'd hit Sandy out in the street, Jericho held his fire, waiting until the men made it outside. The paunchy guy was hanging on to another man, limping badly on his bloodied knee, and the fourth, the skinny one, was clutching his shoulder.

Jericho opened fire, shooting well over their heads to avoid hitting his deputy. An echoing rifle shot sounded from outside, and then nothing. No shots. No cries. No voices. Not a sound.

A shiver went up his spine. What the hell was happening out there?

He stood up, raced for the exit, and pulled up short. What he saw was the worst thing he could have imagined.

Chapter Eighteen

Maddie! What was she doing here? Tucker had her pinned with her back against his filthy shirt, a thick-fingered hand squashed over her mouth. One of Jericho's rifles lay in the dust at her feet.

His belly tightened as if a horse had kicked it. It had been Maddie, not Sandy, who had fired shots at the gang from behind him? He shook his head. Not possible.

Yeah, it was possible. Damn idiot woman! She'd sneaked over to the jail, somehow eluded Sandy and lifted his spare Winchester off the gun rack in his office. Tucker must have maneuvered himself behind her, probably shoved one of his men forward to cover his move and then grabbed her from behind.

Dammit, what did he do now?

She squirmed in the outlaw's grip, her long yellow skirt tangled around Tucker's denim-clad legs. Jericho's mind went numb. He couldn't get off a shot without hitting her.

"Drop your guns, Silver," Tucker yelled over her head. He yanked his arm tighter across her midriff. "I'll kill her if you don't drop 'em!

He had to do it. He couldn't risk Maddie getting hurt.

He tossed both revolvers onto the ground in front of Tucker and then stood motionless, studying the situation. What now?

One of the outlaws lay on the ground, a gaping wound in his thigh in addition to the shattered knee Jericho had given him. A quick glance told him the horses had strayed a few hundred yards into the field behind the mercantile.

"Get the horses, Rafe," Tucker shouted.

One of the men, the skinny one Maddie had winged in the shoulder, started for the field. Purposefully, Jericho moved closer to Maddie, who was still imprisoned by Tucker's scarred hands.

The outlaw tightened his hold. "Stay back, Silver."

Jericho kept walking slowly forward. "You're not gonna shoot me out here in broad daylight, Tucker. Whole town'll be waking up, hearing all this gunfire. That's a lot of witnesses for a murder."

He stopped a scant yard away from Maddie. "Thought I told you to stay out of sight," he intoned, working to keep his voice steady.

She looked into his eyes and his heart stopped. Defiance, not fear, shone in their green depths. And something else—pride. *Pride?* Damn fool woman!

He swallowed hard. Yeah, she'd probably saved his life showing up when she did. But a jolt of irrational fury bit into him anyway. "Dammit, you should have sent Sandy instead."

She blinked slowly. Twice. That must mean no.

Jericho kept talking. "On the other hand, Mrs. O'Donnell, you did me a good turn."

This time she blinked three times. Yes.

Sandy bolted around the corner of the bank into Tucker's view, but before the deputy could aim his rifle, one of the outlaws pointed to Maddie. Sandy looked her way, and the man plunged forward and kicked the weapon out of the deputy's hands.

Jericho sucked in a long, slow breath. Tucker had his hands full holding on to her. The wounded man lay moaning on the ground, and the skinny guy, Rafe, was collecting the horses from the nearby field. The paunchy one had Sandy covered, and another man held a revolver aimed at Jericho's heart.

Could he...?

Nah. Even if he could reach one of the weapons on the ground, he'd be dead before he could lay a finger on it, and Maddie along with him.

"Back off, Silver," Tucker snapped. He tilted his head toward Sandy. "You, too, deputy. Now, soon as Rafe gets those horses over here, we're gonna load up them sacks of gold and ride out. Your lady friend's comin' with us."

Jericho froze. He couldn't let Tucker take her. But how could he stop him?

Favoring his wounded shoulder, the skinny man led the horses to within a few yards of Tucker, and at that moment Jericho made a decision. He couldn't force the issue now, but he had to make sure of something. He moved forward another step and under the cover of jingling bridles, spoke very softly to Maddie.

"You still have that lucky piece you always carry with you?"

Three blinks. Good. She'd remembered. She still had the pistol in her skirt pocket.

Rafe and the paunchy guy each heaved a canvas sack of gold onto the back of a horse.

"What about me?" the man on the ground whined.

"Dusty, you're no good all busted up," Tucker snarled. "I'm leavin' you behind." He lifted his hand from Maddie's mouth and jammed a revolver barrel under her chin.

"Don't say nuthin'," he warned. He jerked his head toward Paunchy, who lashed her hands together with a strip of rawhide, lifted her onto the nearest horse, and attached it with a lead rope to Tucker's mare. He looped the rawhide binding Maddie's wrists around her saddle horn, then the outlaw swung his bulk up onto his own mount.

The other two men gathered up Jericho's two revolvers and both Winchesters, and handed them to Tucker, then hefted the two remaining Wells Fargo bags onto their shoulders and manhandled them up behind their saddles.

The downed man lay cursing in the dust while the three remaining gang members clambered up onto their mounts and galloped toward the open field. Tucker was leading the fourth horse with Maddie.

"Hey," screamed Dusty. "Wait!"

"Fat chance," Tucker yelled over his shoulder. "You kin keep Dipley company in jail."

Clenching and unclenching his fists, Jericho watched the dust rise after them and ground his teeth. He should do something, but what? Wasn't a damn thing he could do without getting Maddie killed.

Just before they reached the edge of the field, Maddie twisted to look back at him and tried to smile. His heart turned to stone. He bolted for the jail, another rifle and a horse. Just as he was about to mount, Sandy stopped him cold with a question.

"You wanna get her killed?"

"Shut up, Sandy."

"No, listen, Sheriff. I know you're itchin' to get her back, but you gotta wait a few hours, let 'em think they can relax. Then go after 'em."

Jericho tried to elbow his way past Sandy, but the young man grabbed his arm. "Don't do it, Sheriff. They'll kill her."

Jericho eyed his deputy, partly with disbelief and partly with respect. He hated to admit it, but Sandy was right.

"How'd you get so damn smart, kid?"

Sandy snorted. "If I knew that, *I'm* the one that'd be the sheriff."

Jericho turned away. "Well, you're not the sheriff." Then he wondered if he was going crazy, and before he could stop himself he made another decision.

"I am going after them. Now."

"Sheriff, you can't. I know you, uh, you didn't get

much sleep last night, but…" Sandy turned crimson and studied the toes of his boots.

Jericho groaned. "You say one word, kid, and you won't even be a deputy!"

"Yessir."

"Now, get Doc Graham over here to tend to that varmint in the street and untie Old Man Warriner inside the bank."

"Yessir."

When he saluted, Jericho thought about slugging him.

He had to do something! He just couldn't sit around and wait. In the next minute he found himself mounted up and setting out after Tucker and his gang.

He got no more than a mile out of town when a shot whined from behind a copse of willows and slammed straight into his calf.

Hell. What now? Should he stop and get Doc Graham to bandage him up? That would give Tucker a couple more hours' head start.

He started to rein in his horse. No, dammit, he'd keep after them. He tried to kick his mount but found his left leg wouldn't work right. And in that moment he knew he'd be worthless unless he could walk.

Sandy was right. He had to force himself to wait, give himself a better chance.

And…though he thought he'd never do this—but that was before Maddie—he'd ask Rooney Cloudman to ride with him. For the first time in his years as sheriff was he really willing to risk someone's life besides his own?

Hell, yes, he was. And keeping Maddie alive was the reason. When he caught up with the gang it would be safer for Maddie if there were two men with weapons instead of just one.

Half an hour later, laid out on Doc Graham's bed on the second floor of the boardinghouse, Jericho closed his eyes and began to plan. First off, he'd tell Old Man Warriner not to worry about the gold. He'd get it back.

And then he'd pray he was doing the right thing and try like hell not to worry about Maddie.

Chapter Nineteen

After six punishing hours with no stopping for rest or water, Maddie gave up trying to sit straight in the saddle and slouched forward to rest her back. Jericho had stopped every hour or so to rest and water his horses, but Tucker spared no thought for his men and animals, driving them on.

She was not sorry for what she had done this morning, grabbing Jericho's rifle off the gun rack at the jail and rushing off to the bank. Her muscles were paying for it now, but it had been worth it. Jericho was alive.

She wondered if she would survive the next twenty-four hours. Oh, she could not think about that now. Instead, she decided to focus on simple, immediate things: the scorching sun on her bare neck, the powdery gray dust blowing into her eyes and up her nose, the sharp catch in her heartbeat whenever she thought of Jericho. If she did not survive this ordeal, at least she had known real passion.

She studied the three men who rode ahead of her. Tucker was big and broad-shouldered, with a florid face and a fat belly that jiggled when he walked. Lefty was paunchy, too, but some years younger than the leader, and he carried his weight better. But he was as cocky as a rooster. His face was marred by a constant scowl.

Rafe, the skinny one she had winged in the shoulder, was tall, red-haired, quiet and odd-looking; his head stretched above his scrawny neck like a giraffe's, and he hawked spit onto the ground so often her stomach roiled.

What a scruffy, godforsaken lot they were. The looks Lefty was sending her were unspeakably rude, but they ceased when Tucker glared at him and muttered, "Hands off."

Another two hours dragged by and she began thinking seriously about how to survive this ordeal. First, she needed to conserve her strength, and that meant getting enough water and food. Beyond that, she prayed the men would not hurt her or—she shut her eyes—molest her.

Or kill her. With her pistol she could protect herself up to a point, but she knew that the instant she fired a single shot at any of them, bullets from three guns would rip into her body.

She thought about dying. It made her think about her life and the choices she had made. When she was young she had let Papa maneuver her into a marriage that almost crushed her spirit and her sense of herself. Joining the Pinkerton agency after she had been widowed had been a good choice; the training had given her self-confidence and a feeling of independence, and the missions she accomplished told her she was doing something of worth with her life.

Only when she met Jericho had she recognized the underlying ache of loneliness. And when he had kissed her, she had become aware of an ache for something else, for connection of one spirit with another, of one body with another.

Oh, heavens, if she died she would never again know that joy.

Tucker called a halt at a shallow stream where the men watered their horses and wolfed down hunks of jerky dug from the depths of their saddlebags. She considered yanking her mount free of the rope tied to Tucker's horse and racing for freedom, but that would be foolish; they would shoot her in the back before she had traveled three yards.

And then she would never see Jericho again.

An hour later they clattered up a rocky hillside and dropped down into a campsite tucked within a circle of jagged rocks. Tucker dragged her off the horse but left her wrists tied. He shoved her toward the fire pit, and she sank her sore, throbbing body down against a smooth-sided gray boulder. Surreptitiously she managed to kick a stick of kindling under the folds of her skirt. If one of the men threatened her, she would use it to scrape hot coals at him.

She patted the small pistol hidden in her side seam pocket, she knew she couldn't shoot all of them, but she could use it on herself if one of them pounced on her.

She dared not think about it.

She eyed the circle of boulders looming around the camp. Jericho would come from the south, but she knew instinctively that he would circle around to… She studied the huge, irregularly shaped rocks. That one, she decided. The gray-green one directly across from her. She patted the lump under her skirt. She would be ready to back him up.

Tucker posted Rafe as a guard, built up the fire, and began to unload the now-filthy Wells Fargo bags. They thunked heavily onto the ground, accompanied by Tucker's satisfied grunts.

"Jest lookit that," Lefty exulted. "And it's all ours, every last ounce of it." He ran his pudgy hand appreciatively over one lumpy bag but did not untie it. "How much you figure's there, Tuck?"

"Enough," came the terse reply. "Rustle up some supper instead of moonin' over our take."

It was a miracle the men did not rip away the canvas to count their treasure. Maddie prayed the men would wait some hours before they dived into their ill-gotten gains—long enough for Jericho to reach the camp.

Tucker slapped a tin plate with two shriveled dust-covered biscuits in front of her. "Eat," he grated.

"I most certainly would if I were able," she retorted. She held up her trussed wrists.

Tucker grunted and sawed through the leather thong with a dull pocketknife. She rubbed her wrists to restore the circulation, gingerly picked up one biscuit and tried to nibble a few bites. It tasted like sawdust.

It grew dark. Lefty replaced Rafe as lookout. Tucker produced a bottle of whiskey, gulped down a swallow and spat. Then he offered the bottle to Maddie.

"Want a pull?"

"Certainly not. I do not indulge in spirits." Except for Rita's brandy-laced coffee. Her mouth watered. How she wished she had some now!

"Churchgoer, huh? Thought so by the look of ya. But ya sure don't handle a rifle like a God-and-Jesus type, little lady."

"My name," she said in a clipped voice, "is Mrs. Madison O'Donnell. 'Ma'am' to you."

"Feisty, too," Tucker muttered. He tossed her a ragged, sour-smelling blanket. "Shut up and go to sleep. We're gonna tally our take."

"I think not," she said quietly but with immense satisfaction. "At this moment the train out of Smoke River is pulling into the Portland station carrying four bags of Wells Fargo gold."

"Couldn't be," Tucker rasped. "We've got that gold right here." He kicked one of the canvas bags. "Slit one of these open, Rafe. Let's see how much we've got."

Rafe pulled a shiny, wicked-looking knife from his boot and started for the bag. Maddie felt for her pistol, still hidden inside her skirt pocket. If one man made a move toward her, she would take out Tucker with her first shot, then aim for Rafe and then Lefty. If she was lucky.

It would be smarter to wait for Jericho, which would even up the odds, but hours had passed and he had not shown up. Was he nearby? Or had Tucker's attempts to cover their trail been successful? Goodness, what if Jericho didn't find her until it was too late?

Rafe emitted a squawk of fury. "Sand!" he shouted. "Nuthin' but sand and gravel!" He turned furious eyes on her. "God, I'll—"

Tucker silenced him with a gesture. "No, you won't. Ain't her doin', it's that damn sheriff. Too smart for his own good."

Maddie tugged the filthy blanket up to cover her smile. Substituting sand for the gold was the one part of her plan that Jericho had adopted. She forgave him for being so stubborn about the rest.

Lefty clumped down from his lookout post, took one look at the sand spilled on the ground and swore in more colorful terms than Maddie had ever heard.

"What're we gonna do now, boss?"

Tucker did not answer. Instead, he stalked over to Maddie and squatted down in front of her. "You knew about this, didn't cha?"

"Yes, I did."

"And Silver knew, too?"

"Yes."

His hard black eyes looked puzzled. "Then why in hell— Why not just let us grab it and ride out. Why try to stop us?"

"Because," she said slowly and clearly, "it is not the gold the sheriff wants. It is you and your gang."

He looked down his bulbous nose at her. "You think a lot of Jericho Silver, don'tcha?"

"Yes, I do." She spoke as calmly as she could. She thought more than *a lot of* Jericho; she knew now that she was in love with him.

"Aw, hell," Tucker spit out. "Women are nuthin' but trouble. I'll deal with you later." He tramped back to his tin plate of misshapen biscuits and left Maddie cold and shaking.

She settled back against the boulder behind her and tried to think about something other than her aching body and the crisp night air seeping through the threadbare blanket.

There was a good chance she would not survive this. In fact, she probably wouldn't. And if she did?

The prospect made her think about her life, about the choices she had made. She was glad she'd met Jericho, glad she had known love, even if it was only for a short while. She blinked back the tears that stung behind her eyes.

Even if she did survive, she knew she could never stay in Smoke River. It was simply too, well, small. It was isolated. Ingrown. It had none of the cultural amenities she was used to, things she had loved since she was a girl.

Worse, she acknowledged, she could not bear to be trapped in a marriage ever again. Marriage was a prison, and a woman's husband was the jailer. A wife obeyed or she died.

She shut her eyes tight. Could there be another way? She stifled an unladylike snort. A lady could not live in sin in a small town like Smoke River. Not only would it ruin *her,* it would ruin Jericho, as well. The townspeople would strip him of his sheriff's badge quicker than a meteor could streak across the sky.

Jericho's whole life was based on serving as Smoke River's beloved sheriff. If he lost that because of her, she could not live with herself.

Jericho reined up suddenly at the sight of the small pile of rocks beside the path—three flat stones carefully stacked on top of one another. An old Indian signal. Thank God! He knew then that he had picked up Tucker's trail.

Rooney Cloudman moved his bay up beside him and stared down at the sign. "Trail marker," he grunted. "Now who d'ya suppose left that?"

"Indian," Jericho said. "Klamath or Nez Percé, maybe. Fellow keeps turnin' up at just the right time."

"You got a scout workin' for you?"

"Nah. Just an unseen friend."

Rooney's mouth quirked. "How'd you manage that?"

"Dunno. Maybe because I've been lettin' him steal jerky out of my saddlebags for the last couple of years."

Cloudman raised both gray-speckled eyebrows but said nothing. Jericho nodded once, and the two men rode on.

Two hours later they came to a muddy creek bank where they could see four clear sets of hoofprints. Rooney leaned forward, propping his hands on the saddle horn. "Looks like she's still with them. Think she's all right?"

Jericho took his time answering. She had to be all right. He would die if Maddie wasn't all right.

"Yeah. She's all right."

"How come you're so sure? There's three desperate men out there, and she's just a woman."

"Maddie isn't 'just a woman.' Maddie is…"

Rooney shot him a look. "Oh, I see. Felt that way about a woman myself, once." He sent Jericho an admiring glance.

"Mind your own business, Rooney."

Rooney cleared his throat. "You thinkin' about marryin' her, Johnny?"

Jericho's throat swelled shut over a lump the size of a lemon. He couldn't answer. God knew he was in love with her, but…

Marry her? Nothing could scare him more. He hadn't mixed with the others at the orphanage, maybe because of his darker skin, his obviously mixed heritage. But he'd been a friend to Little Bear. He'd let her chip through the protective shell he'd thrown up, and after that he'd shared everything with her, confided in her, cared about her.

And then, on that day he'd never forget as long as he lived, he'd watched her die for something he had done. Since then he'd never let himself get close to anyone, never let himself care about another human being. Something about it, about caring and permanence, had left him wary all his life. He was a loner, and he liked it.

Up until now.

"Let's move," he grated.

Without a word, Cloudman reined his mount back onto the faint trail, and for the next few hours they followed it in silence. Jericho scanned the ground ahead and tried not to think about Maddie.

Just when the horses were close to being played out, the tracks petered into dust and Jericho sighted the boulder-protected hideout up ahead. Tucker's camp.

They picketed their mounts half a mile away and crawled on their bellies to lie hidden until the moon rose. They'd have just enough light to spring a trap.

An hour passed, and Jericho began to sweat. When he couldn't stand to wait any longer, he rolled toward Rooney. "Now," he intoned.

As they'd agreed, Rooney circled to the left and disappeared from view. Minutes later, his rumpled gray hat poked up from between two large red-veined rocks. Jericho crept in the opposite direction. He tried not to think about when he and Maddie had pulled the same stunt a week ago and it had gone horribly wrong.

This time he couldn't make any mistakes. At the first sign of trouble, Tucker would kill her.

After a skin-prickling half hour, he saw Rooney's gray hat move up, then down, then up again. Jericho waited and slowly counted to twenty so his deputized companion could crawl into position.

When it was time, Jericho called out.

"Tucker? You're surrounded. Drop your weapons."

Nothing.

"Tucker?"

No answer.

Sweat soaked the neck of his shirt. "Jeb Tucker?"

Cautiously, Jericho stood up, peeked over the rocks, and sucked in his breath.

Nothing moved in the circle of boulders. Shredded canvas bags were strewn among piles of sand; dirt had been hastily kicked over the fire. The camp was deserted.

Jericho kept his rifle aimed at the fire pit and worked his way down through the rocks. Behind him he heard the hammer click on Rooney's rifle.

Jericho hoisted his Winchester shoulder high and scanned the area. Nothing but muddled boot prints and a scrap of leather thong, no outlaws.

"Rooney," he yelled. "Come on down. The place is deser—"

Suddenly a scrap of yellow fabric caught his eye, wedged behind a flat-topped hunk of granite. *Maddie.* His body went cold. He clunked his rifle onto the ground and started toward her.

"Maddie!"

She lay at an odd angle, her face hidden under one arm. "Rooney," he yelled.

"Hell," Rooney breathed at his back. "Is she—"

Jericho grasped her shoulders and eased her body free of the rocks. Oh, God, she… He had to look away. The back of her head was sticky with blood.

"Turn her over," Rooney said quietly. Jericho rolled her over as gently as he could and placed two fingers at her neck. A thready pulse fluttered.

"She's alive." Then he saw the huge purpling lump at her temple.

Rooney knelt beside him. "Don't move her any more, Johnny. She might be hurt inside, as well."

Chapter Twenty

"Maddie? *Maddie?*"

She moaned and opened one eye. The other was blood-encrusted and swollen shut. "Jericho…"

"Maddie, stay with me. Try to concentrate."

All at once he felt a crazy urge to cry. Dammit, men didn't cry! Tears stung at the back of his eyes and he clamped his lips together.

Rooney knelt on her other side and inspected the cuts on her temple and the back of her skull. "Looks like she got slugged pretty hard and more than once. Pistol butt, maybe."

Jericho could only nod.

"Musta thought she was dead. They musta hit her and left her to die."

Jericho wanted to shut Rooney up so bad his fists burned.

Maddie moaned again, but her eyelids remained closed.

He bent over her. "Maddie?"

Her mouth opened and Jericho stopped breathing. "Head hurts," she whispered.

"Maddie, what happened?"

Maddie ran her tongue over her cracked lips. Rooney offered his canteen, and Jericho grabbed it and dribbled water into her mouth.

"Tucker knew you'd follow… Waiting for you." She struggled to get the words out. "Then he decided not to."

"Are you hurt anywhere else?"

"Just my head, I think." She reached her hand to her temple, then touched two fingers to the back of her head. "Ouch! Ooh, that hurts."

"Yeah, someone hit you pretty hard."

"Rafe," she said. "The skinny one." She opened her good eye. "What…does it look like?"

Someone behind him snorted. "Hell, Johnny, if she wants to know how she looks, there's still plenty of life in her."

Maddie recognized Rooney Cloudman's voice and tried to smile.

"Shut up, dammit." Jericho's voice.

"Now don't get riled, Sheriff. There's no need to get so testy. Stop worryin'."

Jericho was worried about her? Again Maddie tried to smile, but her jaw hurt too much.

"I'll bring the horses," Rooney said. "Got some blankets you kin wrap her up in." She heard genuine concern in the man's voice.

"Hurry, dammit!" Then Jericho trickled more water over her lips and she reach up to touch his cheek. His skin felt damp and that made her breath stop. Her chest ached.

Rooney returned with two blankets. Jericho carefully wrapped her up into a cocoon and lifted her into his arms. When she groaned she heard him catch his breath.

"What now, Johnny?" Rooney's voice again.

"Gotta get her on my horse and—"

"I mean about the Tucker gang. You've got an injured woman and a bunch of outlaws on the loose. Got a choice to make."

"Like hell I do," Jericho said, his voice quiet.

There was a long silence, and then she heard Rooney's voice. "I know how you feel, Johnny, but—"

"Shut up, Rooney. This time, Maddie comes first."

The trip back was pure agony. Maddie slept through most of it—or thought she did. Every so often she jolted from comforting blackness into a sharp awareness of pain and Jericho's arms around her. And his voice.

"Hang on, Maddie. Just a few more miles, and we..."

She drifted off before he finished talking. Each time she struggled back to consciousness, Jericho's voice sounded more hoarse. But he kept talking to her.

What seemed like years later he lifted her pain-racked body off the horse and carried her up the porch steps into Sarah Rose's boardinghouse. Upstairs he gently he laid her down on a soft bed that smelled of sun-dried sheets and lavender, then stepped back so Doc Graham could examine her.

Doc pried up one eyelid and studied her pupil, watched her gaze track one finger when he moved it back and forth in her field of vision. Finally he raised his gray-frosted head and held Jericho's gaze.

"What is it you two do when you're not here in my office getting bandaged up?" he snapped. "First you both get shot. Now she's got a head injury worse than any horse kick I've ever seen a body live through. This lady's got one hell of a concussion."

Jericho squeezed Maddie's hand but said nothing.

"Forget I asked," Doc quickly amended. "Everybody knows you're a lawman, Johnny, but what about her? I heard she was your cousin, but you know, I don't really think so."

"Maddie's not my cousin."

"Some kinda law, then?"

"Not exactly," Jericho said.

"Well, what exactly?" Doc barked.

Maddie flinched at his tone, and that set off her headache again. She struggled to keep both eyes open, especially the swollen one, where Tucker had smacked his elbow into the socket when she refused to obey. With the other she stared up into the older man's lined face and opened her lips.

"I am…an actress," she pronounced carefully.

"Sure you are." Doc's voice was full of disbelief.

Mrs. Rose entered with a cup of something, tea, Maddie hoped. She fervently prayed the landlady had added some brandy. What she got instead was a spoonful of laudanum mixed into a cinnamony-tasting brew. At least she didn't have to think up any more lies for the doctor.

The men turned their backs while Mrs. Rose eased her out of her mud-spattered garments and into a white muslin nightgown, then tiptoed out, followed by Doc Graham. Maddie could hear their voices in the hall.

"Maybe Miz O'Donnell is just a greenhorn from back East," Doc was saying. "An unlucky visitor out here who gets herself in deeper than she—"

"Huh!" Mrs. Rose snorted. "You ever see a green-horn with a loaded pistol in her skirt pocket?"

The voices faded.

Jericho returned, pulled a chair up close to the bed and enveloped her fingers in his large warm hand. Even when Sandy clomped up the boardinghouse stairs to report about the jailed prisoners, Jericho did not let go.

"She hurt bad?"

"Bad enough," Jericho answered.

Maddie stopped trying to keep her eyes open and let her lids drift shut. Her limbs began to feel heavy, but her mind felt light and floaty, like soap bubbles. She didn't want to think about anything.

"Sheriff, you think Tucker'll try to break the prisoners out?" Sandy's voice.

"Wish to hell he'd try," Jericho said. "Save me goin' after them again."

"I knew you was gonna say that. I think you've done enough. This time I'm goin' with you."

"Shut up, Sandy. I'm the sheriff."

Sandy expelled his breath in a rush. "You're right about that. You're just about the stubbornest old coot I—okay, Sheriff. Okay. But if you change your mind, I'll be at the jail."

The deputy tiptoed out and Maddie heard Jericho's voice. "And the jail is where you'll stay, my friend."

She fought through the drowsiness and the sickening waves of pain in her temple. "Jericho, promise you will not go after those men tonight."

He squeezed her hand. "Not tonight, no."

"Will you stay here with me for a while? Please?" Her thoughts were all jumbled together like loose pieces of a jigsaw puzzle, but she knew she wanted him here, beside her.

Jericho let out a long sigh. "Sure, I'll stay. Kinda glad we're alone. There's some things I want to say to you."

"What things?"

"This probably isn't the time, but I've been wondering about something." He said nothing more for a few heartbeats, then, "I guess Smoke River's nothing like Chicago, is it?"

"No, it is not."

"Does that matter to you, Maddie? Do you think you could, um, grow to like Smoke River?"

She thought for a long minute. Jericho had always been honest with her; she must be the same. "It does matter, yes. I am not used to small towns. I do not think I could ever get used to living in one."

Another long silence. "You're gonna leave when this is over, aren't you?"

"Yes. As soon as the gang is captured, I am going to leave. Mr. Pinkerton is in Chicago. My detective work is in Chicago, with Mr. Pinkerton."

"You gonna marry him?"

Maddie did not dare laugh; it made her head hurt too much. "Oh, no, I will not be marrying Mr. Pinkerton, or anyone else."

"Why not?" he said after a long hesitation.

"I was married once before and I was very unhappy. It was nothing but endless teas and receptions and afternoon socials. I had no time for myself, for my music and my painting. And my husband did not care about what I wanted. Marriage for me was a trap. The very thought makes my head hurt."

Jericho said nothing, but she heard the hitch in his breathing.

"Besides," she added with a chuckle that made her head throb. "Mr. Pinkerton already has a wife."

"Listen, Maddie," he said, his voice rough. "I don't see things that way. I know Smoke River is a real out-of-the-way place, but…"

"Jericho, stop."

"I can't. Dammit, Maddie, in my whole life I never wanted anyone like I want you."

"It cannot work," she whispered. "We want different things. You want some kind of commitment, and I…" Her voice started to drift off.

"Maddie? What is it you want?"

"I want…well, freedom." *I do want it, don't I? I have always wanted it.*

"Yeah. I guess those are different things."

She forced her eyes open and reached up to touch his jaw. "Jericho, we do understand each other, do we not?"

He looked away. "Yeah, we do. I don't like it, but we do."

Something in Maddie didn't like it either, but at the moment her mind was too cloudy to think why.

Jericho sat by her most of the night, feeling hungry and mad, and shaken in a way he hadn't felt since he was a kid. Maybe he didn't know who he was, exactly, half Mex or Indian or white or whatever. Maybe he wasn't like other men. But he knew *what* he was.

There were some things a man risked his life for, things like peace and justice. And there were some things a man couldn't live without. He felt as if he'd struggled through the blackness of a blinding storm into the light.

And now, dammit, now he wanted one of those things. He wanted to love a woman. This woman. Maddie was fine and strong and so beautiful it made him ache.

Around three in the morning, when his mind was as quiet as he knew it was going to get, he figured out what he had to do.

He slipped down the staircase to the front porch, buckled on his gun belt, checked his rifle and jammed it into the saddle scabbard. Then he mounted and rode out of Smoke River, praying he'd find another Indian marker to show him the trail.

"Alone?" Maddie said in disbelief. She stared at Sandy across the boardinghouse breakfast table. "You let him go *alone*?"

The deputy ducked his head and focused on the brimming coffee mug before him. "You ever try to stop the sheriff from doing anything? Don't mean to be rude, ma'am, but when Sheriff Silver gets a notion in his head he's like a bull buffalo."

"For heaven's sake, this is not simply a 'notion' This is the misguided, foolhardy man who thinks he has nothing to lose."

"Nah, that ain't it. Sheriff thinks he's invincible, like them Roman soldiers in those history books he reads."

Maddie snapped her jaw shut and instantly wished she had asked the doctor for another spoonful of laudanum. The persistent ache behind her eyes was starting in again, and she gritted her teeth against the pain. Against the frustration. Against the fear. Jericho would get himself killed and then she would never know another moment of happiness.

She stood up and found she was unexpectedly wobbly. Sandy bolted to his feet, slapped his big paws on her shoulders and forced her back into her seat.

"Now you listen to me," he ordered. "Jericho don't need you to do somethin' dumb, so you just sit there nice and quietlike 'til he gets back." He gave her a little shake. "You hear me, Miz Detective? Jest let him alone."

Awash with violent, throbbing pain, Maddie let her head droop. She covered her eyes with one shaking hand and tried to calm her thundering heartbeat. Why, *why* did she have to fall in love with a man like Jericho Silver? A man braver than any intelligent human being had any right to be, a wonderful, honorable fool of a man who would do his duty or die.

She became aware of Sandy's hand patting her arm. "Aw, don't cry, Miz O'Donnell. Here." He stuffed a folded handkerchief into her hand.

"I am not crying," she sobbed. "I am th-thinking up a proper punishment for h-him for going off alone."

The deputy chuckled. "Look, ma'am. Jericho's done the exact same thing a dozen times since he's been sheriff. Nobody thought he'd come back alive from his first manhunt, but he's proved us wrong so many times we don't even think about it anymore. He's hard to kill."

"Oh, s-stop talking, Sandy. Maddie wiped her eyes. "*I* am thinking about it. About him getting killed." She scrunched the handkerchief into a ball.

Sarah Rose flew into the dining room, wiping her hands on a flour-dusted blue apron. "Sandy! What on earth did you say to her?"

"Aw, hell…er…heck, Miz Rose. I just explained 'bout Johnny."

The landlady's blue eyes hardened. "She knows all she needs to know about Johnny."

"Yes'm." The deputy gulped a swallow of his cold coffee and bolted for the front porch.

Sarah rubbed her hand over Maddie's heaving shoulders. "You just cry it out, dearie. Then you go on out to the porch an' talk to Rooney. He's the smartest man I know, outside of Johnny."

"J-Johnny is not smart at all," Maddie sniffled. "He is intelligent, but that d-does not make him smart. A s-smart man would not go off alone to…"

She gave up, turned her face into Mrs. Rose's soft bosom and wept until she began to feel dizzy.

"Come on, dearie." The older woman propelled her out onto the veranda where Rooney Cloudman sat rocking in the porch swing. He shoved over and Mrs. Rose eased Maddie down beside him.

"Talk some sense into her, Rooney. She's gone and fallen in love with our Johnny."

Rooney studied her. "Well, you're not the first," he said kindly. "But you sure might be the prettiest." He snagged the sodden handkerchief out of her hand and produced another from the pocket of his fringed buckskin vest.

"And maybe," he confided in a low, raspy voice, "you'll be the last."

Maddie shook her head and blew her nose.

"You're not Johnny's cousin, are ya? Didn't think so. He never knew his ma or his pa, so how would he know a cousin from a trapeze artist?"

Maddie said nothing, just mopped at a new freshet of tears. It was not at all like her to weep, but she could not seem to stop.

"So, don't tell me no lies, ma'am. Who are ya, anyway?"

"I am a Pinkerton agent, Mr. Cloudman. A detective."

He gave her a long, considering look. "That why ya pack a Colt .32 in your skirt pocket? Oh, don't bother denyin' it—Sarah, uh, Mrs. Rose told me about it."

"I was sent to help Sheriff Silver capture the Tucker gang. My job was to gather information and supply Jericho with intelligence. But at the moment I am not feeling like a terribly successful Pinkerton agent."

Rooney flashed her a lopsided grin. "Well, honey-girl, them jobs are always more complicated than they sound. The minute ya start supplyin' intelligence, you're involved way over your britches—er, knees. Ya want to see things work out right."

"Mr. Cloudman, I—"

"Why don'tcha call me Rooney? Seems to me we're gonna have a long and interestin' friendship."

"No, Mr. Rooney," Maddie whispered. "We will not. As soon as the Tucker gang is behind bars, I will be returning to Chicago."

"Chicago, huh?" Rooney tugged on his salt-and-pepper mustache. "Kinda far away from Smoke River, ain't it?"

Maddie nodded.

The beginnings of a frown creased the man's sun-tanned forehead. "Well, that don't make much sense if you and our Johnny—"

She shook her head so violently her headache again bullied its way into her left temple.

"Oh, I see." He rocked the swing back and forth for a full minute. "Well, hell, no, I don't see!"

"Let me explain," Maddie said, her voice quiet. She spoke nonstop for the next quarter hour, telling him everything, even hinting about that night in her hotel room, and all the time Rooney rocked and nodded and pursed his lips. Finally she ran out of breath.

"So it's big-city livin' that appeals to you, huh? Why's that?"

For a moment Maddie could not answer. "Well," she said at last. "Chicago has museums and concerts and libraries and even a university. And it has Mr. Pinkerton."

"Yeah," Rooney muttered, holding her gaze. "Pinkerton's in Chicago, all right."

Maddie plunged on. "My detective work is very important to me. It is always interesting. Each assignment is a challenge. An adventure. As I told you, I had an extremely proper and unimaginative upbringing. And it was terribly dull being married. So I am partial to doing things that are, well, important."

"You like a challenge, do ya?"

"I do, yes. Something that *matters*."

Rooney rocked and rocked while Maddie gulped back tears and massaged her throbbing temple. The soft morning air smelled of honeysuckle and fresh grass, and way up in an alder tree a sparrow chirped and twittered in the quiet. She liked it, all of it. Even the sparrow.

But it wasn't Chicago.

"Well, honey-girl," Rooney finally rumbled. "I hear what you're sayin'. And I hear what you're wantin'. And I've got some thoughts, if you'd care to hear 'em."

"Yes, Mr. Cloudman, I would."

He cleared his throat. Twice. "You ain't gonna believe this. You ain't even gonna like it much, but here it is."

Maddie held her breath. She liked this weathered-looking man beside her. And she knew he would tell her the truth, at least as he saw it.

"Now," Rooney continued. "I know about life, both good and bad." He touched her arm. "And you gotta know I'm on your side, Miss Maddie."

"Yes, I do know that." She patted his rough, callused hand where it rested on his thigh.

"Well, here it is, then. You say you crave a challenge. An adventure. Somethin' worthwhile that really matters."

"Yes, I do."

"Honey-girl, let me tell you, there ain't nothing more challenging or full of adventure or worthwhile than lovin' someone. It's a challenge to get along with someone for years and years, and it's one helluva challenge to keep lovin' a body when you'd as soon dump a bucket of wash water over his head."

Maddie stared at him. This was not what she'd expected to hear. Not at all. And he was not finished.

"Now, I've learned something over the years, Miss Maddie. The best kind of people are the kind you can sit on a porch and swing with. Never say a word, just sit."

He slanted her a sharp look. "But ya know somethin'? Life is richer, and more fun, and more challenging when you love that someone you're swingin' on the porch with. And it's sure as hell empty when you don't."

His bushy eyebrows rose. "Now, you tell me. What has Chicago got to top that?"

Chapter Twenty-One

Maddie filled the long hours waiting for Jericho to return with sewing lessons from Verena Forester. It kept her hands busy so she didn't spend time wringing them until her knuckles cracked, worrying about Jericho.

She cut and sewed a new calico walking skirt with two inseam pockets, one large enough for her pistol, and two daringly cut nightgowns, one in pink silk and one in a delicate pale blue lawn. She even had Verena create a new hat for her—silk velvet with partridge feathers.

Always outspoken about everything, during Maddie's lessons Verena commented on the summer heat, on Carl Ness's shocking addition of ready-to-wear pantalettes to his mercantile stock, even on Sheriff Jericho Silver. "Never talks much. If I didn't know better, I'd think he was half sphinx instead of half Indian or whatever it is he's half of."

Maddie looked up from her pincushion. Whatever

Jericho was, she could not hear his name without a flock of butterflies fluttering into her stomach. The dressmaker shook out a length of red seersucker and laid out the paper pieces of a Butterick dress pattern. "Jericho Silver's been a mystery ever since he turned up in Smoke River."

Maddie kept her head bent and stitched the hem on her blue nightgown. "Is Jericho perhaps a mystery because he doesn't court any of the girls in Smoke River?"

"Huh!" Verena's scissors crunched into the seersucker. "That's true enough. Though plenty of 'em have pined after him. The man is as skittish as a spooked deer."

Oh, no, he isn't, Maddie thought with a secret smile. Jericho was not skittish. When he wanted something, he went after it. What Jericho had done all his adult life was protect himself from emotional involvement.

When she couldn't stand any more of Verena's chatter, Maddie talked Doc Graham into teaching her how to suture cuts, and every afternoon she had tea with Rooney and Sarah Rose on the honeysuckle-swathed front porch of the boardinghouse.

She discovered that Rita at the restaurant had been married not once, but twice—once in Texas and once in Montana. "Awful," the waitress said of Texas. But Montana had been "beautiful." Rita had been a widow for the past twenty years.

"Ain't worth the risk to hitch up with anybody

again," she confessed. "Unless—" she sent Maddie a teasing look "—he looks like Johnny Silver."

Maddie spent a lot of time thinking and she decided the young man she had once encountered at Carl Ness's mercantile was most likely the informer for the Tucker gang; but shortly before she was abducted, the "cousin" disappeared.

The bakery in town, run by a Chinaman everyone called Uncle Charlie, sold the most extraordinary lemon pies. Rooney was partial to them. Mrs. Rose encouraged Maddie to try making her own piecrust and offered her the use of the boardinghouse kitchen. Her initial efforts were tough and chewy, but just yesterday she had produced a crust so flaky it showered tiny bits of pastry all over Rooney's buckskin vest.

But no matter what she did to distract herself, apprehension hovered over her all day, every day, like a veil of worry and questions. One Sunday she even visited the Smoke River community church and found herself bargaining with God. *Please, Lord, please, return Jericho to me alive and I will never ask You for another thing.*

Four more days dragged by, and suddenly Maddie could not bear one more minute of sewing lessons or sutures or lemon pies. That evening at dinner she slumped in her chair at the restaurant under Rita's worried look and put her face in her hands.

I cannot go on this way. I simply cannot. All the life has gone out of me.

Resolutely she lifted her head to glance out the

front window and spilled her cup of brandy-laced coffee all over the tablecloth.

"Jericho!" she yelped.

Rita materialized at her side. "Where?"

Maddie pointed. Rita forgot all about sopping up the spill and joined Maddie at the window.

Four horses moved steadily down the main street. One had a blanket-shrouded corpse slung head down over the saddle. Maddie recognized Rafe's red hair. The second horse carried a pudgy figure with one arm splinted across his chest. Lefty. Tucker lurched along on a black gelding, his wrists lashed to the saddle horn.

And Jericho. Covered in dust, his hair straggling into his eyes, he looked so haggard it brought tears to Maddie's eyes. He moved slowly, as if he had not slept for days, and she gulped back a shaky sob. Her relief at seeing him alive and uninjured drove away her fury at his leaving her without saying goodbye.

She jumped to her feet and headed for the doorway.

"Maddie, wait!" Rita called after her. "What about your steak?"

"Save it for my breakfast. I have to see Jericho!"

Rita propped her hands on her ample hips. "See Jericho, is it? Well now, Miz O'Donnell, that saves me askin' a thousand questions I been wantin' to ask." She removed the dishes from the table and grinned all the way into the kitchen.

Maddie dashed into the street straight at Jericho's gray horse, which shied and sidestepped until he brought it under control. He reined up and sat staring down at her. His face was so dust-streaked sweat ran down in rivulets.

"Jericho! Are you all right?"

"Maddie, don't ever rush at a horse like that. Like to get yourself stomped."

"Jericho." She started to cry for no reason and he leaned down and touched her shoulder.

"Don't, Maddie. It's all over."

"Are you all right?" she asked again.

He gave her a lopsided smile. "I will be. I need a bath and a shave and…" His voice dropped to a murmur. "And then I need to take you to bed."

Her heart flipped over and dropped into her stomach. She gazed up at him and tried to breathe normally. "Come to the hotel," she said. "I'll order a bath for you."

He nodded, then tipped his head at the men behind him. "I got the rest of the gang." Then he grinned, touched his hat brim, and moved on down toward the jail.

Maddie stared after him until he was out of sight and then she raced into the hotel and up the stairs to her room.

Señor Sanchez and his wife lugged hot bath water up to her hotel room and dumped it into a wooden tub. Maddie waited and waited, wondering what kept Jericho, while the water slowly cooled. Disappointment choking her breathing, she watched for him through the window.

Suddenly the door banged open and she gave a little cry. Jericho walked into the room, strode straight to her and wrapped both his arms tight around her.

"Maddie." His voice was hoarse.

He smelled of dirt and sweat and leather. He held her without speaking while his heart thumped unevenly against her breasts. She was so glad to see him she could scarcely speak.

"Jericho," she murmured into his shoulder. "Thank you, *oh, thank you,* for not getting yourself killed."

He laughed and loosened his arms just enough to capture her mouth with his. His kiss went on and on, his mouth hungry, his breathing erratic. Her knees turned to lemon-pie filling.

He broke away and buried his face in her hair. After a long minute he stepped away and held her at arm's length.

"I know I look kinda rough. I came straight from the jail."

"You look simply wonderful to me," she said softly. "I do not care about dust or your four-day stubble or your tangled hair or…anything. Oh, Jericho, I was so worried."

"Yeah, me, too. If anything could go haywire, it did. Had to shoot Rafe when he charged me, and that fat fellow got drunk and slipped off his horse going down the side of a steep canyon. Broke his elbow. Tucker—well, let's just say when the man gets scared enough, he stops thinking. I caught him cold, dropping his pants behind a coyote bush."

Maddie bit off a laugh. "He will never forgive you for that."

"Don't care if he does. Tomorrow morning, the Federal Marshal's takin' him and the other prisoners to the courthouse jail in Portland. Tucker's also wanted in Idaho for killing four miners and stealing their diggings."

"So, it is over?" Maddie dropped her gaze to the carpet to hide her smile of relief. When she lifted her head, their gazes locked. His eyes looked so tired her heart stuttered.

"Jericho?" she whispered.

"Yeah?" He reached for her and at the same moment looked over her shoulder and spied the bathtub. Without another word he stepped past her, unbuttoning his shirt. Then his jeans. His boots clunked onto the floor and his socks sailed through the air to land on top of them.

He circled the tub, stepped out of his drawers, and splashed down into the water. "God, that feels good."

Maddie stared at him. "The water must be stone-cold by now."

"You know how hot it was out there tracking those men? This feels like heaven." He settled back in the tub with a contented groan, resting his head on the metal edge. His eyelids closed.

Maddie studied his sun-bronzed face for a long minute and then looked closer. Heavens, had he fallen asleep?

"Jericho?"

He didn't answer.

"Jericho? Must you go back to the jail tonight? Jericho?"

No answer. Her heartbeat thrummed like hoof-beats against her ribs. She wanted to ease his weariness. Oh, heavens, she wanted to take care of him.

She slipped a folded towel under his neck and laid another within reach. Then she removed her clothes, donned a blue silk wrapper and curled up on the bed to watch his muscled chest rise and fall.

She studied his chin, his neck, the part of his ears that showed under the over-long dark hair, his shoulders, the suntanned arms that lay along the sides of the tub. Even dusted with dirt and mud and bits of leaves he was a beautiful man. She wanted to crawl into the bathwater with him.

She swallowed a giggle. The small tub would overflow and poor Señor Sanchez would have more work to do mopping it all up. She would wait for Jericho to wake up, and then…and then…

Jericho jerked out of a deep sleep, wondering where the hell he was. Then he remembered Maddie and the bathtub and laughed softly. He never thought he'd be so tired he'd forgo Maddie for a nap in a tub of cool water.

The light in the room looked warm and kinda rosy. Sunset, maybe. He glanced out the window where dusk was fading into a purple-blue sky tinged with scarlet. Maddie was propped up on the bed with two pillows behind her and a pretty blue gown hitched up so one of her bent knees showed.

Forget Tucker and his gang. Forget three nights with no campfire and no supper. And no whiskey. Forget that his chin was stubbly and he couldn't keep the hair out of his eyes and his neck was sunburned. Maddie was here with him and that was all that mattered.

He scooped handfuls of the tepid bath water over his body and then dunked his head under the surface. When he came up and opened his eyes, Maddie had not moved. And, heavens, she was smiling at him.

He grabbed a clean towel, hurriedly wiped himself down and rubbed his hair almost dry. Then he wrapped the damp towel around his waist and finger-combed his hair so it wasn't straggling over his forehead.

"Maddie?"

"Yes?"

He lowered his aching body onto the bed next to her.

"In the morning, I'll have to get word to Sandy to bring me some clean socks. And drawers. And a shirt. And—"

"No, Jericho," she said calmly. "You cannot do that in the morning." She brushed the hair out of his eyes.

"Why not?"

"It will have to be in the afternoon."

He kicked the towel onto the floor, stretched out beside her and gathered her close. "Pretty nightgown," he said, smoothing one hand over the blue lawn.

"Do you like it?"

"Yeah." He waited a heartbeat, then reached for the hem. "Take it off."

"But I—"

"Take it off," he repeated.

When she did, he kissed her and touched her all over, just as he'd dreamed of doing for the last four days. "You're mine, Maddie. And I want you like hell." He rolled on top of her.

The first time was urgent and hungry, and left them both near tears. The second time was slow and skilled, and afterward they held each other in silence.

Finally Jericho broke the quiet. "What did you do while I was gone?"

"Oh, lots of things. I baked a lemon pie. Rooney Cloudman likes lemon pies. And I took some sewing lessons—stop smiling!—from Verena Forester and listened to all the gossip about everybody in Smoke River. Even you. Especially you."

Jericho frowned.

"Verena thinks you are mysterious."

"Verena is the busiest busybody in town," he said. "What else?"

"Well, let me see. I did some target practice with Sandy. It scared the jail inmates half to death. They thought we were a vigilante party."

Jericho chuckled.

"Rita Sheltonberg and I are becoming good friends."

"Sheltonberg? That's her last name?"

"That is her last husband's last name. Her maiden name was Kelly."

Jericho kissed her. "You know what, Maddie? I never thought I'd like lying in bed talking to a woman, but I like doing it with you. I like it a whole lot."

"I like it, too, Jericho."

The quiet in the room stretched into soft kisses. Neither of them heard the soft tap on the door.

Señor Sanchez entered quietly. "I come for bathing tub and to bring package from jail man. He say is for the lady."

Without looking up, he laid the parcel just inside the door and began dipping pails of water from the tub.

"Clean socks," Jericho murmured in her ear.

"And a shirt, I hope."

"And maybe a pair of drawers. On second thought," he whispered, "I don't need drawers."

Maddie clapped her hand over her mouth to stifle a spurt of unladylike laughter.

Keeping his eyes on the floor, Señor Sanchez set the buckets of water out in the hallway and backed out the door, dragging the empty tub.

Jericho nuzzled her ear. "You think Sanchez noticed my boots by the door?"

"No. Señor Sanchez is so near-sighted he is almost blind. His wife told me."

"She did, did she? Far as I knew, Señora Sanchez hasn't spoken a word about herself or her husband for the five years they've worked at the hotel."

"Well, perhaps you don't have a Pinkerton lady's touch," Maddie murmured. "She talks to me. Her name is Rosa."

"You're a good detective, Maddie." His voice sounded tight.

"Damn right," she whispered. "I even found out that Sol Warriner has four granddaughters. By Christmas it might be five."

Jericho pulled her back into his arms and pressed his face against her hair. "Maddie," he murmured. "You smell good."

"Jericho, I did something else while you were gone."

"Yeah? Tell me."

She took a slow, deep breath. "I purchased my return ticket to Chicago."

Chapter Twenty-Two

Jericho's head came up and he stared at her. "What did you say?"

"I said I purchased—"

His body jerked. "Maddie. Dammit, I don't want this to end."

She grazed his cheek with her knuckles, moving them slowly over his skin in a light caress. It made his spine shiver.

"It has to end, Jericho. We both know that."

"Hell's half acre, *I* don't know that. You're not wrong a whole lot, Maddie, but you're damn wrong now."

She let out a shaky sigh. "It's not like you to avoid facing things. You're burying your head in the—"

He sat up. "You're the one who's not facing things. You could be happy in Smoke River. I know you could."

She snuggled her head onto his shoulder. "You know no such thing, Jericho. I could be happy with you, perhaps, but not in Smoke River. Just because you—we—want something does not make it necessary."

"*Necessary!* What's not necessary about caring for each other?"

"Being together," she said slowly. "Here, in Smoke River."

"Maddie," he said, his voice quiet. He rested his forehead against hers. "Maddie, marry me, dammit!"

"Oh, Jericho." She tipped her face up. Her eyes were shiny, like two wet emeralds. "A part of me, a very large part of me, would like to do just that. But—"

"But? But what?" His heart twisted inside his chest. He curled his fingers around her shoulders. "I love you. How can you not know that?"

"I do know that," she choked out. "And I love you, too, Jericho. But—but it will not be enough."

"Oh, for—" He bolted off the bed and tramped back and forth in the small room. "You mean the population of a damn town is more important than—"

"It is not the population size. Well, yes, in a way it is. I would have no life of my own here. For a while I would be content to cook and clean and wash and iron like other women in this town, but I could not do that for the rest of my life. I would feel…trapped."

He stood with his back to her, saying nothing. What could he say? Even if God sent down the most eloquent words, it would do no good. She was as immovable as a stone statue.

He worked to control his breathing and closed his hands into fists. "You're wrong, Maddie. I think we've got something that's worth fighting for."

"But it takes more than one, do you not see? In the end I would hurt you, and I could not bear that."

"What the hell do you think you're doing to me now?" he shouted.

"Now," she said, her voice shaking, "now I am just disappointing you."

"It's more than that and you know it."

"No, it is not. Be fair, Jericho. I have a right to a life on my own terms. You have a life here on your own terms. You keep the peace, capture outlaws, help people."

"And that's been enough for a good life," he snapped. "More than enough."

"There's something else, too," she said. Her voice was beginning to tremble. "I have always wanted my freedom."

He opened his mouth, but she stopped his words with a finger against his lips. "And so do you. Not freedom, exactly, but…well, being alone. Being responsible only for yourself."

A crushing black fear barged into his gut. "No, Maddie. No."

"Yes. You keep part of yourself hidden, unreachable. And deep down underneath, you like it that way."

"Up until now." He was so angry he couldn't think straight. "Maybe now I want something else."

"People in Smoke River admire you. They respect you. They look to you for, well, justice."

"Up until now," he repeated. "They might not like me so much if I kidnapped a lady detective. Or…"

He drew a deep breath and tried his damnedest to smile. "If I strangled her."

She let out a quavery laugh. "You would never do such a thing."

He gritted his teeth so hard his jaw ached. "Try me."

For a while there he'd felt pretty good about himself. And about Maddie and himself. He'd bet all the gold that Wells Fargo could bag up that she cared about him.

He gripped her shoulders and gave her a little shake. "Maddie, listen to me." He opened his mouth, then closed it. He couldn't say what was inside. He couldn't do it. He closed his eyes and tried anyway.

"Knowing you, Maddie—oh, hell, loving you—has pushed me to—dammit, I don't know how to say this—to be the man I always wanted to be."

"What could you want to be that you are not already?"

He swallowed. "A man who'd risk admitting that he needed someone. A man who could love someone and not wake up every morning afraid of losing her. I'll fight like hell to hold on to that."

She just stared at him, her eyes shiny with tears, and then her mouth twisted into a soft "Oh." Moisture sheened her cheeks, dripped off her chin.

"I never knew my mother or my father," he said softly. "I could be anybody's kid. But sure as hens lay eggs I'm trying to be my own man. I figured that would be a worthwhile thing in life."

"Yes, it is," she said, her voice quiet. Too quiet. "Oh, Jericho, I don't know what else to say."

"Hell, I feel like I've come in from the cold only to find the damn fire was out. I'm as far away from what I want as an alfalfa field is from the moon."

"Jericho," she sobbed. "I—"

"There's one other thing I want to say to you, Maddie, and you're not going to like it much."

She lifted her face. "Go on."

He took a deep breath. "Grow up, Maddie. You can't have everything just the way you want it all your life. I want you to stay here in Smoke River with me."

"I—I can't, Jericho. I just can't."

They stared at each other a long time. Finally he pulled her into his arms and spoke into her hair. "I don't think I can stand saying goodbye to you with a lot of people watching. I'll meet you at the station right before the train leaves."

Chapter Twenty-Three

In the morning, Maddie steeled herself to say her farewells. The eastbound train left at noon; she donned her pale green seersucker travel suit, packed up her travel valise and walked out of the Smoke River Hotel for the last time. Her mind was clear, but her legs—and her heart—felt as heavy as the iron anvil at the blacksmith's livery stable.

Saying goodbye was more difficult than she ever thought it could be. She had grown fond of the people in Smoke River—some more than others, of course. And she was finding it hard to leave them. The ache in her heart grew worse with each passing hour.

She would miss Rita's raspy voice in the restaurant each morning. She would miss Verena Forester's gossipy fitting sessions and, while she would always remember her sewing lessons, she knew she could never again bring herself to wear the blue nightgown she had made.

Doc Graham's voice was more gruff than usual

when she stopped at Sarah Rose's boardinghouse. "If you ever decide to become a doctor, Maddie, you just skedaddle back out here and take over my practice. I'm gettin' too old to keep sewing up the sheriff."

Sarah Rose bustled out of the kitchen and tearfully folded Maddie into her arms. "You look just beautiful, dearie. And—" she wiped her eyes with her starched gingham apron "—I do admire that marvel of a green hat you're wearin'. What's it made out of, anyway?"

"Silk velvet," Maddie said, grasping the woman's hand. "And partridge feathers."

"You shoot the partridge yourself, did you?" Doc Graham queried. "I hear you're a pretty good shot."

Sarah blew her nose. "As a matter of fact I hear you're pretty good at everything, my dear. Includin' making lemon pies. Oh." She sniffled into her apron. "I surely do wish you'd stay."

Maddie looked into the older woman's kindly face and choked back tears.

Rooney Cloudman rose from his chair at the dining table and planted a kiss on one cheek then the other. He didn't say a word, but his eyes looked suspiciously wet. She kissed him right back on both his whiskery cheeks and whispered the Comanche word he'd taught her for *friend*.

Sandy arrived and swept up her new carpetbag, bulging with the new walking skirts and shirtwaists Verena had made and the two new nightgowns Maddie had sewed herself. And four bars of special lavender soap Mr. Ness had presented to her at the mercantile earlier that morning.

Sandy swung the bag alongside him as he marched her to the station. "Won't be half as much fun without you here, Miss Maddie. And Jericho—"

"Please," she interrupted. "Do not say anything about Jericho right now." Her voice wobbled in a most embarrassing manner.

"Well, it's just that… Well, gosh, it'll be awful dull around here with you bein' gone. If I was sheriff, I'd deputize you in a heartbeat just so you could go bounty-hunting with me."

She gave a shaky laugh. "You are on your own when it comes to bounties, Sandy. I have never believed in them."

The deputy scanned the small crowd at the train station. "Wonder where the sheriff is?"

"He will be here," Maddie said quietly. Oh, goodness, how could she bear to say goodbye to him? Inside her carefully arranged face she gritted her teeth to keep from weeping aloud.

She knew she had to leave Smoke River. She had to, if she wanted to follow her own path, to have the freedom to live the life she had always wanted. But at that moment her throat felt so tight and achy she wondered if she would be able to speak a single word to Jericho when the time came.

Sandy tramped up the two steps to the loading platform. "Here we are, Miss Maddie. Sure do wish—"

She stopped him with a look. He settled her travel bag on the platform close to the shiny iron rails and craned his neck down the tracks, watching for the train.

Against all logic, she hoped it would be late.

Oh, no, she could not wish that. It would just make it harder. She clamped her lips together and fought back a choking sob.

Yes, of course, she did want to return to Chicago. To Mr. Pinkerton and her challenging life as a detective. It was just that, well, it was unexpectedly wrenching to leave Smoke River.

And as for leaving Jericho...

She could not bear to think about that.

She heard the train whistle a long way off, a throaty, mournful cry cutting through the noonday quiet. Sandy peered down the tracks, shading his eyes from the sun. "Here she comes, right on time."

The locomotive, belching steam and plumes of black smoke, chuffed closer. Four sharp toots announced its arrival, and the engine rolled slowly past the platform, stopping with an ear-splitting squeak so the passengers could board.

Sandy stepped forward and hefted her bag onto the bottom step of the landing. Then he turned toward her and stuck out his hand.

"I'd be pleased to shake your hand, Miss Maddie. You sure proved me wrong."

Maddie hesitated. "Wrong about what?"

The deputy's Adam's apple bobbed. "Wrong 'bout a woman not having the sand to be a Pinkerton agent. Far as I can see, you're the best detective anybody could want."

She ignored his proffered hand, stretched up on her toes and kissed his cheek. "And you are a very fine deputy, Sandy. You…you will watch over Jericho, won't you?"

"Oh, sure, ma'am. He'll never know that I been watchin' out for him all this time, and now—"

The sheriff strode down the platform, and Sandy broke off.

Jericho grasped Maddie's elbow and pulled her away from his deputy. Jehoshaphat, he was jealous of any man who came near her.

She was dressed in green, just like that day she'd arrived, and there was some kind of puffy new hat on her head. He hated it. A fluff of veiling and some feathers on a woman didn't protect her from the sun or the wind or…

At the same time he loved it simply because it was Maddie's.

He'd always remember her in green seersucker or whatever that crinkly-looking fabric was. His gut knotted.

God help him, he couldn't do this.

He walked her away from the crowd then turned her into his arms. "Don't go, Maddie," he murmured. "For God's sake, don't go."

She shook her head against his shoulder but did not speak.

The train gave a short warning whistle. Jericho found he could not utter a word, and maybe that was better. Maddie's mind was made up; there was noth-

ing more to say. But in his own mind he refused to
believe he would never see her again.

All at once he snaked out his hand and grabbed
that silly hat off her head. He tried to smile but
couldn't manage it, so he did the only other thing
he could do. He kissed her one last time, a long, long
kiss he knew he'd never forget.

"I love you, Maddie," he whispered against her
mouth. "I will love you till my heart stops beating."

She held him tight for an extra few seconds, then
lifted her hat out of his hands and turned away. With
a flash of white petticoats she climbed onto the iron
steps and vanished inside the car.

His entire being went cold.

Maddie wrestled open the passenger-car door and
sank down onto the nearest velvet-upholstered seat.
She felt wretched. Simply wretched.

She gazed out the window at the main street of
Smoke River with its tidy little stores and the Golden
Partridge Saloon, the Smoke River Hotel where she
and Jericho…

A jolt of agony slammed into her chest. What was
wrong with her? She wanted to return to Chicago,
did she not? She wanted to feel useful and valued
for her professional skill. Wanted to explore libraries and museums, attend concerts, enjoy the opera.
Wanted to…what?

*You can't have everything just the way you want
it all your life.*

Maddie straightened her spine, feeling her backbone grow as rigid as the flagpole in the town square.

Grow up, Maddie. Grow up.

She kept hearing his voice through the buzzing in her head, an insistent, low burr that would not stop.

Oh, for heaven's sake…

It only takes an hour to like someone, some poet whose name she could not recall had written. *And a day to love someone. But it takes a lifetime to forget someone.*

She stood up and pushed her foot a step forward.

The train coupling jolted, and the passenger car began to roll forward. Jericho watched until his eyes blurred, and then he closed his lids against an ache that went all the way down to his boots.

The cars clicked against the rails, picked up speed and began to rattle, but still Jericho did not open his eyes. He couldn't stand watching the train that was taking Maddie away from him fade into the distance and disappear.

The chuffing sound grew fainter and fainter until all he could hear was the low mumble of voices around the station and the cry of a red-tailed hawk overhead. He folded his clenched hands across his body and opened his eyes.

His vision swam and everything looked smeared and indistinct.

Somewhere in front of him a bit of green came into focus. He blinked, swiped one hand across his wet eyes and squinted into the sunshine.

Maddie stood on the other side of the tracks, just stood there, so still she looked like a painting. He must be dreaming.

He gulped in a breath and squinted across the tracks again. Her feathery hat sat slightly askew on her dark hair, and the green striped skirt rippled around her ankles in the breeze.

"Maddie?"

She started across the rails toward him.

He stood looking at her, wondering if he'd gone loco.

"Maddie?"

She released the travel bag in her hand, let it plop down in the middle of the tracks and met him halfway.

"Maddie. Hell, I don't think I believe this."

"Hush." She clung to him, kissed him until he was sure he'd taken a bullet in the brain and gone to heaven.

"Maddie," he rasped against her mouth. "What the hell are you doing here?"

"I should think it would be obvious, Sheriff. I am kissing you."

He choked back a laugh. "Yeah, but why? How come you're not on the train?"

She looked up at him for a long, long time. She sure had a funny expression on her face. A tingle of warmth began to crawl up his spine.

"Jericho, what would you think of a sign over the sheriff's office that says Silver and O'Donnell, Detective Agency?"

He stared at her. "What are you talking about? A detective agency? But that's why you're going back to—"

"Well, yes, it was. But what if my detective agency is not in Chicago? What if it is here?"

"You mean here, in Smoke River? You'd stay in Smoke River?"

With him?

Yes! He kissed her some more. A lot more. Then he stepped back and looked at her.

"Wait a minute," he said in a voice he scarcely recognized. "What about a sign that says Silver and Silver, Detective Agency?"

She reached up to put her arms about his neck and lifted her mouth to his.

"Damn right," she murmured.

And then she kissed him once more, right in front of God and Sandy and all the people gathered at the Smoke River train station.

"Maddie," he finally whispered against her lips. "Let's go back to the hotel. Maybe Señor Sanchez can find a bathtub big enough for the two of us."

She kissed him again. Harder. "Damn right," she said again.

Epilogue

The following Sunday, Jericho Silver and Maddie O'Donnell were married in the Smoke River community church, where they held hands throughout the entire ceremony. Maddie wore a simple blue silk dress with lace at the neck and sleeves which Verena Forester had cobbled up in the two days allowed her. Maddie carried a bouquet of honeysuckle and yellow roses.

Jericho wore his usual jeans, pressed with a crease sharp enough to slice cheese, a dress brown buckskin jacket and a dark blue linen shirt, open at the collar.

Rooney Cloudman walked Maddie down the aisle and stood dabbing at his eyes with a red bandanna throughout the ceremony, along with Deputy Sandy. Sarah Rose stood at Maddie's side and sniffled.

As a wedding gift, Maddie gave Jericho a brand-new set of embossed leather-bound law books and a handsome set of malachite bookends to hold them on his desk.

Before the wedding, Jericho had left town on a

mysterious mission to a horse ranch near Prineville in eastern Oregon. The afternoon of their marriage, he led Maddie out of the church, where she found waiting for her the beautiful palomino mare she had called Sundae.

Maddie and Jericho moved into a pretty little white cottage next door to Sarah Rose's boarding-house, where they started their married life and the Silver and Silver Detective Agency, which is still in operation…

But that is another story.

* * * * *

*Look for CHRISTMAS IN SMOKE RIVER from
Lynna Banning in
WILD WEST CHRISTMAS anthology
Coming October 2014*

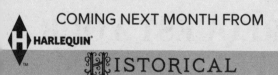

REQUEST YOUR FREE BOOKS!

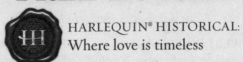

HARLEQUIN® HISTORICAL:
Where love is timeless

2 FREE NOVELS PLUS 2 **FREE GIFTS!**

YES! Please send me 2 FREE Harlequin® Historical novels and my 2 FREE gifts (gifts are worth about $10). After receiving them, if I don't wish to receive any more books, I can return the shipping statement marked "cancel." If I don't cancel, I will receive 6 brand-new novels every month and be billed just $5.44 per book in the U.S. or $5.74 per book in Canada. That's a savings of at least 16% off the cover price! It's quite a bargain! Shipping and handling is just 50¢ per book in the U.S. and 75¢ per book in Canada.* I understand that accepting the 2 free books and gifts places me under no obligation to buy anything. I can always return a shipment and cancel at any time. Even if I never buy another book, the two free books and gifts are mine to keep forever.

246/349 HDN F4ZY

Name	(PLEASE PRINT)
Address	Apt. #
City	State/Prov.	Zip/Postal Code

Signature (if under 18, a parent or guardian must sign)

Mail to the **Harlequin® Reader Service:**
IN U.S.A.: P.O. Box 1867, Buffalo, NY 14240-1867
IN CANADA: P.O. Box 609, Fort Erie, Ontario L2A 5X3

Want to try two free books from another line?
Call 1-800-873-8635 or visit www.ReaderService.com.

* Terms and prices subject to change without notice. Prices do not include applicable taxes. Sales tax applicable in N.Y. Canadian residents will be charged applicable taxes. Offer not valid in Quebec. This offer is limited to one order per household. Not valid for current subscribers to Harlequin Historical books. All orders subject to credit approval. Credit or debit balances in a customer's account(s) may be offset by any other outstanding balance owed by or to the customer. Please allow 4 to 6 weeks for delivery. Offer available while quantities last.

Your Privacy—The Harlequin® Reader Service is committed to protecting your privacy. Our Privacy Policy is available online at www.ReaderService.com or upon request from the Harlequin Reader Service.

We make a portion of our mailing list available to reputable third parties that offer products we believe may interest you. If you prefer that we not exchange your name with third parties, or if you wish to clarify or modify your communication preferences, please visit us at www.ReaderService.com/consumerschoice or write to us at Harlequin Reader Service Preference Service, P.O. Box 9062, Buffalo, NY 14269. Include your complete name and address.

HHI3R

SPECIAL EXCERPT FROM

HARLEQUIN®

HISTORICAL

*Meet one of four deliciously **Dangerous Dukes** in the
first installment of Carole Mortimer's new miniseries.*

*Read on for a taste of the
darkly seductive and irresistible*
ZACHARY BLACK: DUKE OF DEBAUCHERY…

Zachary raised his head to look at her with mercurial
grey eyes. There was a flush to the hardness of his cheeks
and his dark hair was dishevelled. "I have forgotten nothing, Georgianna," he assured huskily. "If anything, I find
that edge of danger only makes you more intriguing.
Besides which, if you are a spy, then you are currently
an imprisoned one. My imprisoned spy." He smiled his
satisfaction with that fact.

Georgianna drew her breath in sharply as she once
again felt the soft pad of his thumb caress across the hardened tip of her breast.

"Perhaps that was my plan all along?" She tried to
fight the sensations currently bombarding her senses:
pleasure, arousal, heat. "Has it not occurred to you that
maybe my plan is to stab you at the dinner table with
a knife from your own ducal silver dinner service?" she
persisted breathlessly even as she found it impossible not
to arch once again into that marauding mouth as it continued to plunder the sensitive column of her throat.

"No." Zachary smiled against the fluttering wildness
of her pulse. He might have become slightly blasé these
past few months, but he was nevertheless positive his

self-defence skills were still as sharp. "Because I very much doubt you will find the opportunity. Or, if you did, that my strength would not far outweigh your own."

"Then perhaps it is my intention to hide one of the knives and take it back upstairs with me, so that I can stab you later, while you sleep?" There was now an edge of desperation to Georgianna's voice; she simply couldn't allow this to continue.

Zachary deftly released the first button at the throat of her gown. "Then I will have to ensure that the door between our two bedchambers remains locked at night."

"I do not believe you are taking me seriously."

"When I am holding you in my arms and about to kiss you? No, you may be assured I am not taking your threats seriously at all, Georgianna," he acknowledged gruffly.

"Zachary!"

"Georgianna," he chided gently as he released the second button and revealed the top of the silky smooth skin above the swell of her breasts.

"I cannot… This is not—" She broke off abruptly as Zachary claimed her mouth with his and silenced her protest.

Don't miss
ZACHARY BLACK: DUKE OF DEBAUCHERY
available October 2014 wherever
Harlequin® Historical books and ebooks are sold!

HHEXP0914

HARLEQUIN®

HISTORICAL

Where love is timeless

COMING IN OCTOBER 2014

Wild West Christmas

by

Jenna Kernan, Kathryn Albright and Lynna Banning

Curl up with a cowboy this Christmas with these three heartwarming tales:

A Family for the Rancher

by Jenna Kernan

Two years ago, Dillen Roach fell for wealthy debutante Alice Truett.
Now she's at his door with his orphaned nephews in tow!
Could Alice be the perfect Christmas gift for this solitary rancher?

Dance with a Cowboy

by Kathryn Albright

Kathleen Sheridan is determined to leave the tragedy of her past
behind her—including brooding cowboy Garrett. But with
Christmas magic in the air, can she resist the warmth of his touch?

Christmas in Smoke River

by Lynna Banning

Gale McBurney is an utter mystery to rich "city girl" Lilah Cornwell.
But to make Smoke River her home by Christmas, she'll have to let this
rugged cattleman take the reins…

Available wherever books and ebooks are sold.

HARLEQUIN®

HISTORICAL

Where love is timeless

COMING IN OCTOBER 2014

Betrayed by His Kiss

by

Amanda McCabe

In a city of shadows…

Orlando Landucci knows all too well what darkness lies beneath Florence's dazzling splendor. And when his beloved sister is torn from him, he will stop at nothing to avenge her death.

…only a kiss can light up the darkness

But from the moment he lays eyes on innocent Isabella Spinola, something inside him shifts. She is the kin of his sworn enemy, yet he feels compelled to protect her. With every forbidden kiss, Orlando's sense of betrayal deepens, so when the time for vengeance comes, will their bond be enough to banish the shadows forever?

Available wherever books and ebooks are sold.

Love the Harlequin book
you just read?

Your opinion matters.

Review this book on your favorite
book site, review site, blog or your own
social media properties and share
your opinion with other readers!

Be sure to connect with us at:
Harlequin.com/Newsletters
Facebook.com/HarlequinBooks
Twitter.com/HarlequinBooks